The Girl in the Tower

J. Sun-Park

This is a work of fiction. Names, characters, businesses, places, events and incidents are either the products of the author's imagination or used in a fictitious manner. Any resemblance to actual persons, living or dead, or actual events is purely coincidental.

THE GIRL IN THE TOWER

Copyright © 2016 J. Sun-Park

Printed in the United States of America

First Printing, 2016

1

"Welcome, welcome. Please, sit down."

Grant took a seat and looked across the table at the man that had invited him to this place, wondering what his intentions might be. The e-mail that had suddenly appeared out of the blue gave him few details, save for the location of a coffee shop for the meeting.

"I'm David Teller," the man said, extending his hand in a friendly handshake.

"Grant Adams," he replied, taking the proffered hand and studying his counterpart as he did so.

He looked to be much older than Grant, probably in his mid-fifties. His black hair was flecked with greying spots, his face showing worn lines of age. His black suit, however, was orderly and neat, fitting him perfectly. Probably a custom-tailored one, and of fairly expensive material at that.

"Thank you for meeting with me today," David continued. "I wasn't sure that you would respond to my message, but there weren't very many ways to get in contact with you. You're a very hard man to find."

"That's by design," Grant replied carefully. "But from what you said in your e-mail I assume that you know my history?"

He nodded. "Yes, it wasn't very difficult to find, in fact. You're a person of some notoriety. Or infamy, as it were."

"Quite," Grant replied, not certain what else to add.

"I would like to hear your perspective on your situation," David said.

"Isn't it all there for everyone to see? Everyone seems to know about what happened."

"Everyone seems to know about what they *believed* had happened," David replied. "But the actual truth could be very different. So do you have a different perspective?"

Grant let out a breath. "OK, where do you want me to start?"

"Where it all began, of course. If you prefer I can ask questions and you can answer them to the best of your ability."

"That might be best."

"Well then. According to my research you started an investment firm fresh out of college with two of your peers. A bold move. Some might say reckless."

"That's correct."

"And how were things at your new firm?"

Grant leaned back in his chair. "Successful. One of my partners already had some connections, which helped. We were able to attract clients and do good business. Everything seemed to be going smoothly. Until it wasn't."

"Ah. Yes. And then your firm ran into trouble, I see. Embezzlement charges. The kind that would even make me wince, even as an experienced professional in the field."

"Yes, those happened," Grant said with a grimace. "They happened, and I should have been more involved. I trusted my partners with the books, and they hung me out to dry."

"What exactly did they do?" David asked.

Grant looked straight at him. "As far as I could figure out, they started running a Ponzi scheme behind my back."

"And you didn't notice?"

"I should have. Auditing finances wasn't my responsibility, but I should have noticed it anyhow."

"What was your role?"

"My role was client relations. I was the one who talked to them directly."

David nodded. "I see. And that would make it very easy for you to not notice what was going on behind the scenes. At least, not until the cracks began to show. When did those occur?"

"When I went to make a withdrawal on behalf of a client and found out there wasn't enough money. The next thing I knew the firm's account was completely empty and my partners were nowhere to be found."

"And then your story becomes a matter of public record," David said. "Investigated by the federal government, exonerated from any wrongdoing, but permanently disgraced by your association with the firm that defrauded so many people. In your current position you'll never be able to get another job in your field."

Grant didn't respond, but he knew that to be the truth. No one was going to take a risk on someone that carried that kind of baggage with them, even if he had been found innocent of any wrongdoing. The stigma of his failure still haunted him.

"And here you are today. If I'm not mistaken you were also forced to file for bankruptcy?"

"I was."

"I see. And you still have obligations toward your student debts?"

"Yes."

"Quite the quandary you're in. Which, of course, is why I believed you might be interested in meeting with me. I believe I have something that I can offer you."

Grant nodded. "Yes, I think so."

David looked across the table at him. "I represent the Arno Corporation, a major business conglomerate that is interested in recruiting you for a corporate position."

Grant frowned. "Um, may I ask why? We just went over why I'm considered to be unhireable."

"To most firms, yes. You carry a lot of baggage with you of the kind that they will never be willing to touch. But this is different."

"What's the position?"

"The personal assistant of Evelyn Arno, one of the minor officers in the Arno Corporation. Are you familiar with them?"

"Yes."

It was hard not to be, since they had control over a variety of business interests. Oil, factories, railways, construction and a myriad of other industries. He knew the patriarch of the group was one of the most wealthy men in the world.

"Excellent," David said. "I imagined you would be, since you've had your hand in the business world. And there are few places in that world where the Arno Corporation does not touch."

"You said that I'm being recruited as a personal assistant," Grant said with another frown. "That seems... unusual. Why would I be recruited for that kind of positions when there's others with better qualifications?"

"You seem hesitant."

"This seems way too good to be true," Grant retorted. "You've told me how much baggage I'm carrying with me from my last failure. And yet I'm somehow being picked for this position?"

"I know this may seem unusual," David told him. "But this was taken under due consideration. It was my understanding that you were personally selected by Ms. Arno herself for evaluation."

Grant wasn't sure how to respond from that. Too many questions were swirling around in his mind.

"I'm still not certain about what this entails, but I'm interested, at the very least," Grant said.

David smiled slightly. "Good. Very good. My task was to gauge your interest and to answer any preliminary questions you might have. Now that we have completed that task..."

He reached down and opened up his briefcase, withdrew a large envelope and handed it to Grant.

"Please make sure that you do not lose any of that," David told him. "That contains your itinerary for the next few days. Will you be able to fly out of here within the next day?"

Grant nodded.

"Excellent. If you could be ready by 9 AM you will be picked up and taken to the airport for a chartered flight. From there you will be brought to Ms. Arno for a final evaluation."

"May I ask what that includes?"

"Oh, it's nothing concerning. Just an informal interview, so your prospective sponsor can get a good sense of your personality. You need to be able to coexist, after all."

"And may I ask what the duties of my job will be?"

"That is a question for Ms. Arno to answer. The specifications for each are different, and I do not wish to mix them up."

"I understand."

David closed the briefcase and stood up. "And now our business concludes. Thank you for your time and consideration. I will see you tomorrow at the appointed time and place. And please, make good use of the contents of the package. Ms. Arno wants you to be well-dressed for your interview."

Grant stood up as well and shook his hand. As David left he sat back down and opened the contents of the package.

There was a printout detailing the itinerary for the next day, an overview of the Arno Group...

And an envelope full of cash.

Grant tried not to swear aloud in shock as he discretely counted the bills. He hadn't been expecting to receive any money, but the total completely stunned him.

Five thousand dollars.

He could feel his mind reeling in confusion. What was going on here? What had he just involved himself with?

And at this point, did he really have a choice?

David was right on schedule with a taxi, picking up Grant in front of his modest apartment and then heading for the airport. A short while later he was on the charter flight headed south.

He made some idle conversation with David for a bit, but then his mind began to wonder about his current situation. Even after a night's rest he couldn't still wrap his head around the stack of bills he had been given.

They were in his luggage, none of it spent on new clothing. Grant still had a good selection of suits from his time as an investment broker. As instructed he had packed three days worth of them, as well as some other assorted items of clothing. No use getting new clothes when the older ones suited him just fine.

But the money wasn't the primary thing bothering him. No, it was the entire situation surrounding him. Why had he been chosen for this? The Arno Corporation was prestigious, powerful. Why would they take a risk on someone who was clearly a liability?

And Grant was exactly that. He may have been cleared of any wrongdoing, but his failure still ate away at him. There was no way that he could wash the stain away anytime soon, not after so many people had lost considerable sums of money. Merely being a part of the firm had tainted his reputation, perhaps permanently.

Why? Why had he been selected for this? The question wouldn't leave his mind no matter how hard he tried to push it away.

A car was waiting for them when they arrived at the airport. A few minutes later he could see the city rising in front of them, dozens of skyscrapers reaching up into the clouds.

"I trust you read your itinerary?" David asked.

"I did."

"Good. What will happen is simple enough. You'll meet with Ms. Arno once we reach our destination. After that everything is up to her discretion."

"Will I have time to change?" Grant asked. He was wearing casual clothing at the moment, nothing more than a t-shirt and jeans.

"That will be up to your host. You of course have been provided with accommodation, so it shouldn't be any trouble. But again, that is up to the discretion of Ms. Arno. Who can tell what she's thinking at any point," David said with a slight smile.

"Is there anything that I should know about her?"

"Nothing out of the ordinary. She is a typical young woman of her age and stature."

Grant wasn't quite sure what he meant by that but was too afraid to ask. He didn't want to appear clueless. At any rate he believed he could adapt to whatever was asked of him.

The rest of the ride passed in silence. As they pulled up to their stop Grant tried not to gasp at the sight. He stepped out of the car and looked up.

The tower stretched up into the sky, faced with a charcoal-colored veneer. Grey granite steps lead up to the entryway, circling around a piece of abstract metal artwork in the midst of a fountain. Grant didn't even bother trying to guess the number of windows in the place. He had seen plenty of impressive buildings in his time, but none so imposing as this.

"Welcome to Eden Tower," David told him. "This will be your accommodations for the time being, and if you should accept your position your permanent residence."

Grant nodded silently, unable to say anything more. He had read the part where accommodations would be provided for him, but the notes had been scarce on details. He hadn't been expecting something so... grand.

He was so lost in the amazement of it all that he didn't notice the other person that had joined them.

"Welcome to Eden Tower," he said, startling Grant a bit.

"Um, yes. Sorry. Thank you," Grant replied awkwardly. He had lived in a big city before. He had seen plenty of skyscrapers before. Why was he so out of sorts?

The man gave him a smile and offered his hand. "I'm Sam, one of the porters for the tower. Good to meet you."

"I'm Grant. Pleased to meet you as well," he replied, taking the handshake.

Sam seemed pleasant enough, his friendly face framed with neatly cut black hair. His navy blue suit was in perfect order as well. Grant guessed that he was a bit older than him as well, probably in his early thirties.

"Porter may not be the best descriptor," David said. "To put it in feudal terms Sam may be better described as a steward of sorts. If you have any concerns about your accommodations he is the person you can ask for anything and everything."

"I aim to please," Sam said with a grin.

"Would you be so kind as to show Mr. Adams to his quarters."

"Of course." He turned to Grant. "Follow me, please.

One of the other porters will bring your luggage up shortly."

Grant fell in behind him as they made their way up the steps, his mind swimming. Quarters. Not a room. Quarters. What exactly was waiting for him in there?

The entryway might be even more impressive than the exterior, stretching up for the equivalent of several stories. The floors looked like they were made of black marble, the walls of some silvery metal. It was impressive, but to him it felt stark, felt… cold.

Sam led him across the lobby, waving to their pair at the front desk and then pressing the button to the elevator.

"I was given instructions by Ms. Arno that I'm to relay to you," he said.

"Oh?"

The pair stepped inside of the elevator, and Sam pressed for their destination in the midst of a whole mess of buttons.

"Ms. Arno requests that you change into business attire of your choice. A suit, preferably."

"Of course."

"It doesn't have to be immediately. You'll have a bit of time to settle in. You'll be meeting with her at 1 PM, so that should give you about thirty minutes to get yourself prepared."

"OK, thank you for the warning."

"Don't mention it. And again, if you need anything just come find me. You can call down to the front desk for me and they'll search me out."

"Thank you for that."

Sam grinned. "No need to thank me for that. It's my job, after all."

"It's just second nature at this point," Grant shrugged. He hesitated for the moment. "Um, is there anything I should know about Ms. Arno?"

"I'm sorry, but I can't tell you that. She specifically told me not to answer that type of question."

"I see. Sorry for bothering you."

"Not a problem. Of course you'd be naturally curious, and I can't blame you for that," Sam grinned. "But I don't think you're going to run into trouble. You were personally recruited, after all."

Grant didn't say anything after that. Once the elevator stopped at their floor Sam led him out and to a doorway. He took out a keycard and swiped it, then handed it over to him.

"Don't lose this, please. Changing the door codes is a bit troublesome. But I'll let you settle in."

Grant stepped inside the doorway and tried not to gawk as Sam closed the door behind him.

Quarters. It wasn't a room or even a suite. To all appearances he had just stepped inside something the size of a house, and a lavish one at that. A hallway stretched out in front of him, with doors lining each side. Like the lobby below the floor was coated with black marble. He walked forward, toward the open end of the hallway and suddenly found himself in the midst of an even larger room.

That was when he realized the ceiling was much higher here. Grant turned around to see a spiral staircase leading up to a loft when the next story would be. He saw several more doorways in the wall at the back of the loft as well.

Quarters. Not a room. Quarters.

The surroundings impressed, but Grant felt even more unease. What had he done to warrant this?

After a bit of exploring he found the bathroom and decided to take a quick shower to freshen up a bit. He wanted to put forward his best appearance, after all.

His luggage was by the bed in the loft when he climbed out and dried off. Grant quickly shed his bathrobe and selected a suit, then put it on.

He checked himself in one of the bathroom's tall mirrors, making sure that he was properly groomed and dressed. Black suit, white shirt and black tie. Short trimmed brown hair. Clean-shaven face. Grant checked his eyes in the mirror, hoping they weren't bloodshot from lack of sleep. Brown pupils and no sign of red. Good enough.

He adjusted his tie, stepped out of the bathroom and grabbed the wristwatch he had placed there. Grant idly looked at the time. 12:59.

"Oh great," he said, hurriedly jogging down the spiral staircase and down the hallway. Just what he needed, to be late at at time like this.

Grant still in the midst of the hallway when he saw the knob turn. At first he thought it was Sam coming to get him, or maybe David. He slowed down to a walk, trying not to appear frantic.

But it was neither of them.

Grant stopped in his tracks as the door opened and a woman stepped through. She wore a simple blue dress and had her long blonde hair tied into a braid. He guessed she was younger than him, probably in her early to mid twenties.

His heart skipped a beat as she looked at him and smiled. "Thank you for coming all this way."

And once again Grant was at a loss for words.

2

The new arrival giggled. "It looks like you're completely nonplussed," she said.

Grant found his voice. "I'm not. It's just..."

"Just what?"

"Just that I was expecting someone different."

"Am I not to your liking?" she asked with a coy smile.

"Well, no, that's not it. I mean, I was expecting one of the others to come get me to take me where I belong."

"Ah, I see. Sam, perhaps?"

"Yes, he was one. Um, Ms..."

"Ms. Arno."

Grant was taken aback for a moment. "Oh. I didn't think..."

"Think what?"

"I wasn't expecting you to come get me in person."

The coy smile still hung on her face. "Well, I was bored,

so I decided to come here myself. Right in the nick of time too, I see. I hope I gave you enough time?"

"Yes, it was plenty."

"Well then. I expect you have questions. If you'll come with me," she said, motioning for him to follow. "I imagine that you haven't had lunch either."

"No," he admitted.

"Good, because neither have I, and I'm not good on an empty stomach."

Their dining room was on a lower floor, a small room set for two. Grant tried to keep his stomach from growling as he took a seat. He had only eaten a bagel early in the morning.

Servers brought in a small assortment of food: soup, followed by a main course of chicken and vegetables. One offered him wine, though Grant refuse. He wanted to keep his wits fully about him for this.

He also noted that the server didn't offer Evelyn any either.

"I've heard that you have many questions about what you're doing here," Evelyn said.

"I do," Grant replied, trying to keep uncertainty out of his voice. It wouldn't do to seem hesitant.

"Naturally. Well, it's like David told you. I'm in need of a personal assistant, and you happened to interest me."

"May I ask how you even found out about me?"

She smiled. "Oh, I have my sources. And you're not

exactly an unknown either. Anyone in business circles is bound to recognize your name."

"Yes."

"And about that. I find your circumstances unfortunate. A consummate professional, done in by backstabbing partners without a warning. A reputation tarnished without any warning. It's enough to give even hardened hearts pause."

"I see."

She laughed. "So stoic."

"Is there any other way to act about it?"

"Oh, you don't have to put up a front for me. If you're going to serve as my personal assistant you're going to be around me a lot, which means I'm eventually going to find out if you're masking anything. So why bother hiding it now?"

"I see."

"Can you only give two word answers?"

Grant looked her in the eye. "No."

"Touché," she replied with a laugh. "And a bit of wit as well. Good, very good. I'd hate it very much if you were actually a bore."

"Thank you, I think?"

"Oh yes, that's a compliment. Some of the other personal assistants I've had... Well, let's just say that they were sorely lacking in the amusement department. It was so dull around them."

"So what does being your personal assistant entail?" he

asked.

"Ah yes, I suppose you want to know that. Well, it's just as it says. You'll help me keep track of my appointments and schedule, and accompany me wherever I need to go. Don't worry, though. It's not extensive. Most of your work is merely a formality."

"A formality?"

"Yes, you'll be doing everything that I described, but it won't be frequent. I hardly have anything to do with the management of the Arno Group. My position is little more than window dressing at this point."

"So why do you need a personal assistant?"

"Trying to talk yourself out of the position, I see."

He shook his head. "No, it's just..."

"Just what?"

"If you're not involved in the group then why do you need to go through the trouble of getting an assistant? Can't someone else serve for the times you need one?"

"Ah, but that won't do. I don't need to have one. I don't need to live in a gigantic tower in the middle of the city either, but I do. And for the times I need an assistant it's good to have one on retainer."

"I see."

"Back to the two word answers, I see," Evelyn replied with a smirk. "Well then, do you think you can handle this? Are you qualified?"

"I can do it."

"But? I think I hear a but in there."

Grant took a breath and then spoke. "Why was I picked for this? I feel like I'm a bit overqualified for this. And then there's all the baggage that comes with me, which you know about."

"I know. I really don't care either."

"That's… unusual."

"Hm, maybe. I like your selection of suit, by the way. I trust that the amount given to you was enough to cover?"

"I didn't spend any of it," Grant said. "This is one of my own suits. The envelope is still in my bag."

She smiled. "Oh? And what were you planning on doing with it?"

"I was going to return it. I tried to return it to David when he picked me up, but he refused."

"And that's why I don't care," Evelyn said. "If you were a liability like everyone seems to fear you probably would have run off with the entire amount. But you didn't."

"I didn't feel like it was right, that's all."

"Ah, so we have a young, skilled broker who can't get another position simply because the perception of him is wrong, through little fault of his own," Evelyn summarized. "So tragic. And yet, I think I can help with that."

"By employing me?"

"Yes, by that. And not just by the benefits you're receiving now. You may be tainted now, but with several years working for the Arno Group will wash that stain away."

"Even if it's just a fluff position."

She gave him her coy smile again. "Well, they don't

need to know that now, do they? So what do you say?"

"You're awfully quick to hire me. And I'm still not entirely sure why you're selecting me."

Evelyn pushed back her chair and stood up. "Walk with me, please."

Grant stood up and followed her out of the dining room into one of the halls.

"You're wondering why I decided to look for someone like you when anyone I pull off the streets will do. I get that," she said. "But I have my reasons."

"Are you willing to elaborate on them?"

"Depends on if you're willing to hear them or not."

"Of course."

She fixed him with an icy smile. "You may regret that answer."

"I'll take my chances."

"That's one reason. Many people would take that as a threat and start cowering," Evelyn said. "But you're willing to keep pushing. I don't need someone around me who continually kisses my feet and tells me how wonderful I am."

"Are there others?"

"Well, clearly you have something inside of your head, otherwise you wouldn't have been nearly as successful as you were. Exempting treacherous partners stabbing you in the back, of course."

"Thank you?"

"And then there's one last thing."

"Which is?"

"You're very pretty."

Grant wasn't sure how to respond to that statement.

"Um, I guess that's a good thing?"

"From your perspective it is. I may not have chosen you otherwise."

"If you wanted someone pretty there are probably better looking men than me," he said. Grant didn't think he was ugly by any means, but he wasn't a supermodel either.

"That may be true, but the prettier the man the less in his head, and I'm fairly certain that being around one for long periods of time would drive me insane by now."

"I guess I'll take it?"

"There's one last thing that needs to be cleared before you can accept though," she said. Evelyn stopped in front of a door and waved her hand in front of it. Grant heard the electronic lock beep and then unlock.

She led him inside the doorway and through a darkened hallway. Grant followed close behind, trying not to lose her. Evelyn made a turn and then headed up a flight of stairs, motioning for him to follow.

Light suddenly cut through the darkness. Evelyn backed away from the lamp she had turned on and sat down on something.

"There's one thing that needs to be cleared with you before you can become my personal assistant. Or secretary, if you prefer," she said.

"What is this place?"

"My room."

Grant looked at her in confusion. Then the realization hit him like a wave.

"Oh. *That* kind of secretary."

"Is *that* kind of secretary more to your liking?"

Grant tried to respond, but his words came out in a stammer. Too many things were happening at once.

Evelyn slid over to him and grabbed his tie, then gently pulled his face down level to hers.

"What's wrong? Am I not attractive enough for you?"

"That's not it," he stammered out.

"Or maybe you don't know what you're doing, hm? Are you a virgin?"

"That's not it either," he protested, feeling the blood rush to his face.

Evelyn let go of his tie and let out a long laugh. "Ah, that certainly got a rise out of you." She composed herself. "But there you have it. That's the one thing you need to be clear about."

Grant didn't respond.

"You can make your choice now. If you refuse I won't be angry. You can simply spend the night, then fly back tomorrow morning and we both can pretend this never happen. Or you can accept and stay."

He still didn't respond.

"So. What will it be?"

Grant felt his mind spinning. This? Staying here and being nothing more than a plaything for her? The though embarrassed him.

But…

But she was right. Everyone was right. This might be his only chance to redeem himself. And if that was the case…

"I'll stay."

Evelyn gave him a smile. "Good. Now come here."

Grant moved toward her and then sat down beside her. He felt Evelyn's hands on him, fumbling with his clothing.

"So unhelpful," she chided him lightly.

He let out a sigh and slipped off his jacket, then his tie and shirt. As soon as he was undressed a hand pressed down on his chest, and then he felt her skin pressing up against his.

"My, my," she said. "For someone who seems so reluctant about this you sure don't have trouble getting it up."

He saw her laugh. "What?"

"The look on your face is priceless," she told him with a smirk. "So many conflicting emotions there. You look so confused right now."

Grant grunted in response.

"Oh, going silent?"

"This wasn't exactly what I was expecting."

"Isn't that a good thing? Isn't this every man's dream?"

"The novelty of it doesn't seem as great in person," he said.

"And yet you stayed. Are you regretting that decision now?" she asked.

"Maybe a little."

"You still have a choice. You can walk out of here and we both forget anything that happened."

He grunted again. "I've made my decision."

Evelyn gave him a smirk. "Well then, let's see what you can do."

Grant noticed how wet she felt as she slid onto him. Evelyn put her hands on his shoulders and started to rock her hips back and forth.

"No help, huh?" she asked with another smirk. "Am I really not that attractive to you?"

"That's not it," Grant said. "But I didn't put a cond-"

"It's fine. I'm on the pill," Evelyn told him.

"That's not foolproof."

"Well, then that just works out to your advantage, doesn't it?" she grinned at him. "But I think we'll be fine. Pull out before you finish if you're so worried about it."

Grant didn't respond.

"So that's it then? You're just going to sit there and make me do all the work?"

He said nothing.

"Lie back and think of England, huh?"

"Huh?"

"Oh, I'm sorry if you didn't get that reference. I-"

"I know what it means," he interrupted her angrily.

"Well then. Is that how it's going to be? If you're going to stay then why not try to enjoy yourself a little?"

Grant scowled and put his hands at her sides. "Fine

then," he told her, and pushed up with his own hips.

Evelyn grunted and then looked back down at him with another grin. "There you go. Isn't this a lot better than lying there flat like a board?"

"Are you just going to spend the entire time mocking me?"

"Maybe I will. It's rather amusing."

Grant had no response but to continue thrusting. He felt his heart racing, his chest heaving more and more by the second. Evelyn's thighs squeezed around him tighter and tighter...

And then the feeling of release swept over him.

"That was fast," Evelyn commented, apparently amused.

Grant looked up at her, panting from exertion. "It's been a while."

"For all that you were going on about it, you didn't even bother to pull out," she grinned at him. "Maybe it wasn't as big of a deal as you thought?"

"I just... forgot."

"You mean you got too caught up in it all."

Grant closed his eyes and sighed.

"What's that for? Truth be told, you're rather selfish. Getting off like that without even trying to pleasure your partner. Are you actually a virgin? Were you lying, and this was your first time?"

He opened his eyes. "No. Are you just going to keep doing this? Because it's going to get old really fast."

She laughed. "Well, perform better in bed and then I can't really complain about it, can I?"

"So do I fail?"

"I'll give you a do-over. Since you've already had your release that should mean you'll last longer this time, right?"

Grant could only shake his head in response.

3

It was all just a dream.

Grant rolled over and slowly sat up, trying to purge the sleepy haziness hanging over him. Yesterday couldn't have happened. It was all just a dream. He'd wake up and find himself back in his own bed, in his normal life.

But as the blurriness faded he found himself in the loft, sun streaming through the windows.

He pushed himself up, climbed out of bed and headed into the bathroom to freshen up a bit. He wasn't dreaming. He wasn't dreaming, but everything seemed so surreal.

Grant turned on the faucet and splashed cold water onto his face, trying to wake himself up and clear his mind. Too many thoughts sat jumbled inside. Was this it? He'd been brought here as little more than a kept man.

"What the hell," he said under his breath, and then he laughed.

He couldn't complain about it. He had chosen to stay here, chosen to go along with her whims.

Grant heard the faint sound of his phone going off and left the bathroom. He picked it up from the nightstand to see a message from Evelyn.

Come to my room when you wake up.

Grant quickly found a pair of pants and a t-shirt as well as a pair of slippers, then put them on. He put his watch on as well and glanced at the time.

8:30.

What did she want right now?

"Don't tell me you want to screw this early in the morning," he muttered to himself.

He texted a message back.

I'll be there in a minute.

Grant quickly made his way down the hall and to her room. He was just about to ring the bell when the door swung open. Evelyn stood in the doorway, her hair unkempt and clad in long t-shirt.

"That was faster than I expected," she commented, motioning for him to come in.

"What were you expecting?"

"That you'd sleep in this morning. You were pretty tired after our little escapade last night."

Grant scowled.

Evelyn shot him an amused glance. "Oh please, you enjoyed it. All four times, I might add."

"Yeah, and I'm still sore."

"It's the good kind of sore, isn't it?"

"I'd really like it if you didn't make it worse," he replied, ignoring the last comment.

Evelyn led him up to the loft and sat down on the edge of her bed.

"And what would you say if I wanted to have some fun right now?" she asked.

"I'd say you're a nymphomaniac," Grant told her.

Evelyn laughed. "And yet you can't seem to resist me."

"Did I have a choice?"

"I *gave* you a choice. Every time, and you didn't take one of them," she retorted.

"This time I might actually take it."

"Well, too bad. You don't get a choice this time."

Grant groaned. "Seriously?"

Evelyn leaned back onto the mattress, a wicked smile on her face. "Consider this a performance evaluation. Whether you can perform under pressure."

"That's not funny."

"I think it is, and isn't that the opinion that counts?"

Grant let out a frustrated breath and moved over to her. Evelyn sat up and pushed him onto his back, then straddled him.

"You should be able to last a while this time, right?"

"That's if it doesn't turn black and fall off."

She laughed. "Is that a comment about me being ice cold?"

"Take it as you will."

"That's an appropriate phrase."

She reached down to his waistband...

And stood up, laughing.

Grant set up. "What the hell was that?"

"Ah, you should have seen the look on your face," she smirked.

"Did you seriously just do that to troll me?"

"You were going to go through with it. All the complaining and you were still going to go through with it," Evelyn told him with an impish grin. "What does that say about you?"

"You didn't give me a choice."

"You say that, but again, every single time before you were given a choice you didn't take it. Can you really say you'd react differently if you were given a choice?"

Grant looked away. "So all that was to just troll me? You called me over here just for that?"

"Of course not. That was just an interesting little diversion," she said. "Today officially starts your first day as my personal assistant. And that means there's things to do."

"What kind of things?" he asked warily.

She laughed. "Not the kind of things you seem to be worried about. I want to go shopping today, which means you'll need to accompany me. And I think you could use an extra outfit or two."

"Maybe."

"Oh, so now you're switching to one word answers?"

"Not this again."

"Fine then. At any rate, you'll need to be ready to go by 11. Meet me back here by then."

"Any instructions on what to wear?"

"Something good-looking but casual. No need to get dressed up like yesterday."

"Got it."

"Good. Now if you'll excuse me, I'm going to take a shower," Evelyn said, pulling off her t-shirt.

Grant stiffened. She wasn't wearing anything underneath.

"Really?"

"Oh don't act like that," she said in an amused tone. "You seemed to appreciate the view last night."

"Is this going to be a habit?"

"Maybe I should make it one," she said.

Grant stood up. "If there's nothing else I'll leave you here to take your shower."

"There's nothing else."

Grant nodded and turned to go.

"Unless you want to join me?"

He turned around and saw the impish grin on her face.

"I'll pass, thanks."

"Oh, so you *do* have some self control in there?"

He couldn't think of a retort. Grant simply shook his head and descended down the stairs. He had other things to do before they left.

Grant got breakfast from the kitchen on the lower

floor, then headed back to his room to clean up before their departure. After a shower and a quick shave he sorted through his luggage, trying to figure out what to wear.

"Good-looking but casual," he muttered.

What would fit that description? He glanced at his phone for the weather report. Sunny, highs in the mid-sixties. Grant sorted through the assortment of clothing and selected a red polo and a pair of khaki pants. He put them on and looked in the mirror. Good enough. Evelyn would probably let him hear about it if they didn't meet her standards.

He glanced at his watch. 10:40. Ready with time to spare.

I'm ready to go, he texted her.

I'm ready too. Come over, she replied.

Grant headed back over to her room.

"Is this suitable?" he asked when she opened the door.

"That's passable, but certainly nothing to write home about," she said. "We can probably do better."

"I'm not sure what you're thinking of, but I might not be able to afford what you're thinking of."

"Oh come now, that's not going to be a problem. Follow me."

Evelyn guided him into a side room that looked like some sort of study and grabbed something off the desk.

"This is yours," she said, handing it over.

Grant took the object and looked down. No mistaking it. Evelyn had just handed him a credit card.

"Um, thanks?"

"That's paid off monthly, so you won't need to worry about it. Just make sure you stay within the limit, otherwise you're not going to be able to buy anything with it."

"What's the limit?"

"Twenty-five thousand dollars."

"What do you think I'm going to spend that much on?" he said.

"Oh, something might catch your fancy. Just remember to stay within the limit and you'll be fine."

Grant took out his wallet and slipped the card inside. "I'll keep that in mind."

"And now you're ready to go. I'll call down to the front desk and have them prepare a car for us."

"Where are we going?"

"Wherever we want. Or more precisely, wherever *I* want."

"Welcome," the shopkeeper said as they entered the boutique. She brightened up as she saw Evelyn. "Ah, Ms. Arno, welcome back."

"Thank you," Evelyn replied with a polite smile.

"Your order came in yesterday. Would you like me to ring it up?"

"I have a bit of other shopping I'd like to do before then, thank you. Do you have any suggestions?"

"Is there anything specific that you're looking for?"

Grant stood off to the side, unsure of what to do. So far

all the stores they had visited sold only women's clothing, leaving him with little to do except watch and carry bags.

There were plenty of those, truth be told. After seeing the total from the first store and almost fainting he decided to stop looking. At this point he was probably holding over ten thousand dollars worth of clothing.

The district interested him, though. Grant had seen plenty of the type in well-to-do places, selling upper-end clothing and luxuries that most people couldn't even dream about. Even when making a good living as an investment broker these kind of prices would have made him wince. But Evelyn? She treated them like they were nothing.

"Bag man," he muttered to himself under his breath. After so many years in college and more trying to build a profitable investment firm this was not where he thought he was going to end up.

Even worse, his current position paid more than his best years at the investment firm, and that wasn't including his suite or the credit card. Apparently sleeping your way to the top wasn't just reserved for Hollywood.

"You're smiling."

Grant realized Evelyn was talking to him. "I am?"

"You didn't even notice? Is something funny?"

"Just thinking about the absurdity of my current situation."

"Why, because you're a man?"

"That's not what I-"

"Whatever." She held something out. "Carry this for

me, OK?"

Grant took the bag and added it to the to the collection. "I hope you're not planning on many more stops?"

"Just one, and it's for you," she told him as they left the store. "After that we'll drop off the bags at the car, and then go to lunch."

"Sounds fine."

"Back to the two word responses, I see."

"Are you just saying that to get a rise out of me?" he asked.

"Well it seems to be working, doesn't it?"

"Let's just go."

Barely twenty four hours later and she was already driving him crazy.

"I noticed that you let me pick out your outfits," Evelyn commented at the restaurant.

"I wanted to make sure that you approved of them. That's all," he shrugged.

"Do you hate any of them?"

"Why would I hate any of them?"

"Obviously you have your own tastes. If you hate them then you should say something about it."

"They're fine," Grant told her. "Some of them weren't what I would have normally picked, but I don't hate any of them."

"Well, that's good to hear. I hope you're not trying to

humor me."

"What would be the point in that?"

She laughed. "Oh, you're not in the mood to suck up to me?"

"You told me not to put up a front."

"That's right, I did. It's so much more interesting when I can know what you're thinking. But enough of that. Take the time to enjoy yourself. Have a drink, if you want."

"Isn't that frowned upon on the job?"

She laughed. "As long as you can walk under your own power I don't care."

"What about you?"

"I'm not going to, of course."

"How come?"

"I have my reasons."

Grant decided not to ask any more and changed the subject. "Any reason you chose a Japanese restaurant?"

"Oh, because I think you should try something. Like sea urchin, or eel."

Grant scowled. "Are you just making me do things for your amusement?"

"Maybe I am," she said with a grin.

"I've had urchin before."

"Well, you can order it if you want."

"So I actually get a choice."

"Of course. You *always* get a choice, you just seem content never taking it. But I'm not going to force you to eat something you don't want."

"So why pick here?" he asked.

"Because I like Japanese food, of course. No other reason."

"No other reason, huh?"

"Well, sitting at a traditional table is a little more interesting than your normal restaurant," she said.

They had had a small room, furnished with a low table and cushions on each side. It felt odd sitting on the floor with no back support, but the cushion was comfortable enough.

Once the waiter came he selected a tuna roll along with a beer. At the rate this day was going he was probably going to need it.

"Not feeling very adventurous, I see," Evelyn commented.

"At least I didn't ask for a California roll."

"Yes, at least that," she said.

"So is this it?" Grant asked.

"Pretty much. Like I said, you accompany me wherever I want to go. Sometimes I feel the urge to get out and do something, but staying home in Eden is fine most of the time."

"Are you the only one that lives there?"

She laughed. "What, and have a whole gigantic tower all to myself? I'm not quite that wealthy."

"I take that as a no?"

"And you'd be right. My siblings live there as well. You'll probably meet them sometime. I'll certainly have to introduce you."

"Have to? Am I some embarrassment?"

Evelyn shot him an annoyed look. "Of course not. Why would I take you out in public if you were an embarrassment?"

"OK, so..."

"It's just… It's just that I don't exactly have the closest relationship with my sisters. Or half sisters, actually."

"Half sisters?"

"You're not familiar with my father, are you?"

"Not about his private life."

She nodded. "Fair enough. He's been married three times, divorced twice. Josephine and Rosalie are from his first marriage, Miranda is from his second."

"And you're from his third, I take it?"

"That's correct."

"So you don't have a connection with your sisters?"

She sighed. "It's not that I hate them or anything. Josephine and Rosalie are twenty years older than me, and Miranda is twelve. It's kind of hard to get over that much of an age gulf. And our interests don't quite match. I have a fairly good relationship with Miranda, but there's still the age distance."

"I see."

"Do you have any siblings?"

"One. An older brother."

"And are you close to him?"

"Fairly. Or I was."

"Was?"

Grant frowned. "How should I put this? Brody and I were close growing up, but there's a bit more distance because we weren't able to see each other as much when we were adults. I went to New York, he became a family man."

"But the connection is still there?"

"Yes, I think it is."

"Then you should be thankful for it. Some people aren't so lucky to have something like that."

Their server arrived with their order. Grant felt his stomach growl, awkwardly trying to eat his meal with a pair of chopsticks. Evelyn seemed to have far better dexterity with them.

"You know," she said after the had finished, "there's another reason why I like this restaurant."

"Oh?"

"The tables are very thin and easy to reach across."

"What does that have to do with any-"

And then he felt a hand slip inside his pants.

"What are you doing?" he asked, barely able to keep his voice steady.

Evelyn didn't respond, instead turned to one of the restaurant staff who was passing by the doorway. "Excuse me. Check please?"

"Right away miss."

Grant felt her hand shift again.

"Now, aren't you in a bind?" she said. "Don't make too much of a scene, because wouldn't that be embarrassing?"

"What the-"

She pressed a finger to his lips. "Shh, don't make a scene. You don't want to humiliate yourself in public, do you? Especially someplace where we might come back to, hm?"

Grant felt her hand shift. "Is this all just a game to you?" he said through gritted teeth.

"Now now, don't be like that. Or I can make this even harder for you, can't I?" She moved her hand again. "My, for how much you're protesting you seem to be enjoying this. Maybe you want more?"

"You're crazy. Uhh," he grunted as Evelyn started to move her hand back and forth.

"Like I said, you seem to be enjoying yourself."

Grant saw the server enter and tried to keep a straight face. Evelyn handed over a credit card, showing no signs that anything was amiss.

He breathed a sigh of relief once the server left the room.

"Thank God."

She gave him a devilish smile. "Why? You're not done yet. He still has to come back with my card."

"Are you going to keep this up until then?"

"I think I might. But don't make a mess. You can wait until we get back to Eden, can't you?"

Grant gritted his teeth again and desperately tried not to think about the hand down his pants.

"And there it is."

"There what is?" Grant asked, looking up at Evelyn.

She smirked at him. "What happened to all the complaints about being sore? You sure didn't seem to be feeling any ill effects. Or am I just that good?"

Grant could feel her hands on his chest in a dominant position. For a moment he felt like shoving her off in frustration, but he held it in. It wasn't like she had held a gun to his head, after all. He had gone along with her game despite himself.

"How long are you going to keep this up?"

"Keep what up?"

He scowled. "Could you cut the games for just one minute?"

"Maybe they amuse me too much. You seem to be enjoying them as well."

"So is this it? We do nothing all day but go random places and screw?"

"Living the dream, huh?"

"Stop it."

She giggled. "There's not a lot of conviction behind that, is there? What you say and what you do are two very different things."

"Why are you doing this?"

"I need some way to amuse myself, don't I?" Evelyn said. She rolled off of him. "Truth be told, you're amusing. Much more amusing than some of the others I've been with."

Grant scowled again and remained silent.

"Such a dark look," she said, running a hand along his cheek. "Well, if you're so against it all I won't force you to stay. You can still back out now, if you want."

Grant remained silent.

"Oh, what's this? Once again as soon as I give you the option to refuse you don't take it. Perhaps you like it this way, hm?"

He pushed himself up.

"Is that all you need from me?"

"Aw, not one for pillow talk?" she said tauntingly.

"Is that it?"

"It's fine," Evelyn told him with a wave. "I don't have anything planned for the rest of the evening, so do with it what you will. Unless I get bored, that is. Maybe I'll call you over."

"If I decide to come," Grant said, putting on his clothing.

"Oh, you will. I think you've already proven that plenty of times."

He could do nothing else but scowl as he left the loft.

4

"Time for you to earn your pay as a personal assistant," Evelyn told him a few days later.

"Haven't I been doing that?"

"None of that is official, dummy. This is going to be part of your public job."

Grant straightened up in his chair, a fine leather seat with plush cushions. "And what exactly am I supposed to do?"

"You're going to accompany me and keep track of my itinerary," she told him. "You have the tablet and everything?"

"Yes," he confirmed. It had been placed in the suite's study along with a myriad of other office supplies.

"Then you have everything you need. You just have to remind me."

"Where are we going?"

Evelyn hesitated for a moment. "We're going to Texas. Arlington, to be specific."

"Arlington? What's in Arlington?"

"The Rangers."

"And what do you have to do with them?"

"My father owns the team," she said. "Apparently there's some big public relations thing going on, and he wants his family there. Have to project the perfect image so all the world can see."

"You sound bitter about it," he observed.

"Maybe I am."

"Any reason?"

"I always have my reasons."

"Any reason that you'd like to share with me?"

"Why do you want to know?"

"So I know whether I need to duck and cover or not."

That at least got a hint of a smile from her. "You won't need to do that. Probably."

"Probably. Do you not like baseball or something?"

"Or something."

"Is it your father?"

She fixed him with an icy look. "You know, you seem to have a lot of questions today."

"I'm just trying to do my job, and I need to know as much information as I can for that," he protested.

In truth he liked that fact that he had managed to turn the tables on her. For once she was the one on the defensive.

Evelyn scowled. "Look, I don't have a close relationship

with my father. That's all there is to it. I don't exactly enjoy being around him, so this isn't some joyous occasion."

"But yet we're going?"

"Yes, because there's no choice."

"No choice."

She fixed him with another icy look. "You don't refuse the Arno patriarch."

"I see."

Evelyn abruptly stood up. "Good. We'll leave tomorrow morning for the airport and take a private plane to Arlington. Be ready. Oh, and you're going to meet my sisters tomorrow."

"Understood."

"I'd prefer it if I did the talking around them."

"Why?"

"Because I don't want you to accidentally say anything wrong," she said.

Grant raised an eyebrow. "Is it really that bad?"

"Once again, I have my reasons."

"OK. I'll be ready."

"Make sure you are," Evelyn told him, then out of the living room and down the hallway.

Grant looked up at the ceiling and sighed as he heard the door close. He could only imagine what kind of disfunction had made her turn out like this.

Grant made one last check in the mirror, making sure that his clothing was in proper order. Grey pants and jacket, blue tie, white shirt, just as Evelyn had requested. Good enough, though he hoped they wouldn't be outside for too long. The weather in Texas was in the eighties today.

He made his way down to the study to collect his tablet, then headed to Evelyn's room. As he turned he saw her walking down the hallway toward him.

"Perfect timing," he said.

She scowled. "There's no perfect timing today."

Grant said nothing, not wanting to provoke her foul mood even further. He fell in beside her as she walked past.

"Hopefully they'll be ready once we get to the bottom floor," she said. "If not we might have to wait, and that's not going to make him happy."

"Wouldn't it have been simpler to go to Arlington yesterday so there's less of a commute?"

"I wanted to do that, but the others didn't want to leave until today. So we're stuck here until then," she said. "Because of course. Can't pull themselves away from their dreamworld for five seconds without them throwing a fit."

Grant wasn't sure he wanted to ask.

"Anyhow," Evelyn said as she pressed the elevator button, "you're going to meet my sisters and my father today. He's especially interested in you, for whatever reason."

That surprised him. "Seriously?"

"He asked that I bring you along," she shrugged. "Why that is I have no idea. I find in unsettling."

She wasn't the only one.

"But here's your chance to get in good with one of the

big players," Evelyn said. "You're not going to have to do much anyhow, other than to accompany me. Do you like baseball?"

"I played in high school," Grant told her. "And yeah, I'm a fan."

"Good. That gives you plenty to talk about," she said. "Saves me from talking to him as well. That's your job, OK? Keep him busy."

"Why?"

"Because I said so."

The elevator opened and they stepped inside.

"No, I meant why don't you want to talk to your father?" he asked. "I know you said you weren't close, but this seems a little extreme."

Evelyn caught his gaze and fixed him any icy glare, worse than any of the others he had seen. Grant imagined this was what a rabbit felt like when being sized up by a wolf.

"Did I say that I wasn't close to him? Well, that's wrong. Truth his, I hate his guts, I can barely stand to be in the same room as him, so I'd like to avoid something that turns my stomach that much, OK? Is that clear enough for you?"

He looked away. "It's clear."

Grant heard her sigh. "Good. Now let's not speak any more about this, OK?"

"Fine with me. I get it," he replied, wondering what kind of treatment her father had inflicted upon Evelyn to make her feel this way.

The rest of the elevator ride passed in silence. As the doors slid open Grant saw several people standing in the lobby, apparently waiting for them.

"Well, you're early," Evelyn commented as she walked to join them.

"Oh, and good morning to you Evie," one of them said.

Evelyn was quickly surrounded by a pair of women, in their mid thirties to early forties by the look of things. Both had brunette hair, and their faces showed signs of cosmetic surgery.

"You're always the one complaining that we aren't on time, so we decided to change it this morning," the other said. "So now who's late today?"

"Like I said, you're early."

"Oh yes, Michael woke me up early today to make sure that I got here on time. So there's that."

The first one turned her attention to Grant. "So this is your new man, hm? Looks like the strong, handsome type."

Grant thought he saw Evelyn try to disguise another scowl.

"Pardon me, I should have introduced you all. This is Rosalie," she said, indicating the first one with shoulder length hair. "This is Josephine," she said next, looking at the second one with longer hair.

"And your name?" Josephine asked.

"Grant."

"And lastly," Evelyn cut in, the scowl now evident on her face, "lastly is Miranda."

Grant looked at the final one that hadn't spoken to him yet, a woman in her early thirties with pale skin and black hair.

"Pleased to meet you," she said in a quiet voice.

"And you as well."

"Oh, how rude, we should introduce our assistants as well," Rosalie spoke up. "This is Michael," she said, looking at the tall, black-haired man hanging further back.

"And this is Corey," Josephine said, pointing to the sandy-haired man next to him.

"Pleased to meet you both," Grant said to them. They both nodded back politely.

"And I have no personal assistant," Miranda said with an easy smile. "I don't require one."

"I see."

Grant saw Sam approach the group from the direction of the front desk.

"You ride will be here shortly," he told them.

"Thank you," Evie replied.

"You weren't at our gathering a few nights back," Rosalie commented to Evelyn after Sam had walked away. "What day was that?"

"Tuesday," Corey spoke up.

"Yes, Tuesday. You haven't been coming at all."

"I was busy," Evelyn shrugged.

"That's what you always say," Josephine chided her. "You need to loosen up and have some fun. You don't want to be a hermit like Miri, do you?"

"Being alone has its benefits," Miranda said, the smile still on her face.

"Too lonely for my tastes." Josephine looked at Grant. "Maybe you can do some convincing," she said to him.

"Maybe," Grant replied, trying not to say anything that would get him into trouble.

Maybe not speaking at all would serve him better. Right now Grant felt like he had stepped right into the middle of a den of vipers.

"So, where did you come from?" Corey asked once they were seated aboard the plane.

"Sorry?"

"Oh, I may have worded that weird. I mean, how did you come to be here?"

"He was probably recruited, same as us," Michael said from his seat facing them.

Grant wasn't sure how to respond. He thought that he'd be with Evelyn for the trip, but she had been pounced on by her sisters at the first opportunity and was in a different part of the charter flight. He had been put in the back of the plane with the other two.

Just his luck, being stuck with two complete strangers in a completely unfamiliar situation.

"That's about right," Grant responded. "I was recruited and ended up here. I guess you went through the same thing?"

"Yeah, you could say that," Corey said.

Michael nodded. "Of course. What else would have happened?"

"What were you before you came here?" Corey asked him.

Michael interrupted before he could start to speak. "Oh, you don't know?"

"Know what?"

"He was involved in a scandal with his investment firm. Lost millions and was investigated by the government."

Corey looked back over at him. "Um, how are you not in prison now?"

"I wasn't responsible," Grant shrugged, trying to put a calm front forward. Inside, though, he could feel his stomach turning in knots.

"Oh, I know that you were exonerated, but that still must have been quite the embarrassment, right? Getting hit out of the blue by your partners? Not to mention having it plastered all over the news," Michael commented.

Grant nodded in response, not sure what else to do. Why was he bringing this all up? Did it even matter?

He saw Corey scowl. "There you go again, having to be a jerk. Do you really have to do that?"

"Just making conversation," Michael said, looking out of the window like nothing was wrong.

Grant said nothing, but Michael was rubbing him the wrong way, and he was fairly sure it was on purpose. But why? Was it just some way to stroke his ego? Was he trying to hurt Grant somehow? If so then why try this way? His past wasn't exactly a secret.

"Don't mind him," Corey said. "He's just doing all this for his own amusement, that's all. Don't know why, but you can pretty much ignore him."

"Huh, now who's being the rude one?"

"Well, you usually deserve it."

"It's fine," Grant said, trying to put an end to the argument.

He leaned back in his seat and closed his eyes, wishing he could be almost anywhere but here. Hopefully he could at least get a quick nap. If not, this was going to be a long, awkward flight.

"Thank God that's over," Evelyn said.

Grant agreed with her silently. He had dealt with plenty of talkative people in his time, but the incessant chatter from Josephine and Rosalie in the limousine had been enough to drive him completely crazy. Coupled with Michael's statements during the flight and the trip had been a thoroughly awful experience.

Evelyn's reaction had been more unsettling to him, though. Through the limousine ride to the airport, the flight and then the ride from the airport to the stadium she had stayed relatively quiet, in completely contrast from her usual outspoken personality.

The change disturbed him quite a bit. She had said that she hated her father, but did he have such a strong hold on her that the mere prospect of seeing him was enough to make her cower? Or was there something else at play.

"So, what's on the schedule for me?" she asked, breaking into his thoughts.

Grant opened up the itinerary. "You'll be making an appearance before the game with the rest of your family."

"For family day," she said. "You're lucky you can go hide in the owner's suite."

"It's only five minutes. Oh. And you're scheduled to MC during the seventh inning stretch during one of the giveaways."

"Great. Of course I get chosen."

"Who else would they choose?" Grant asked. "Um, don't take this the wrong way, but out of the four of you you're probably the best qualified for it."

"Because I'm still young and sexy?"

"Not how I would have put it, but yeah, let's go with that."

Evelyn shook her head. "And that's probably what my father is thinking too."

Grant wasn't sure how to respond and said nothing.

"Well, since you're not doing anything else except reminding me when I need to go you might as well get settled in. Come on."

She led him out of the side office and toward one of the elevators.

"Where are we headed?"

"The owner's suite."

Evelyn lead him out of the elevator a few floors up and

led him down the hallway. She stopped at a doorway flanked by two security guards, who opened the doorway for them.

"And here we are," she said as the doorway closed behind them.

Grant looked around the room, impressed by the scene. Right in front of them sat several chairs and couches, made of fine leather and emblazoned with the Rangers logo. A bar and buffet sat off to one side, both empty at the moment. Further down the room three rows of cushioned chairs sat facing a wide windows, giving them a perfect view of the ball field. If that wasn't enough there were several screens around the suite as well.

"Well, this is better than the nosebleed seats," he said.

"Just a little," she replied, a slight smile on her face.

Grant stepped forward to the window and looked down over the field, watching a few players go through their warmup routine. Finally something he recognized. The past week had been so... frantic, so disconnected from his previous life.

He heard the door open behind them and turned, expecting to see one of Evelyn's sisters entering. It was none of them.

Instead, an older man with a strong, stern look on his face stepped into the suite. Grant saw Evelyn stiffen out of the corner of his eye.

"Father," she said.

"Evelyn." He turned toward Grant. "I assume this is your new assistant?"

"It is."

He walked down to meet him and extended his hand. "Robert Arno."

Grant took the handshake. "Thank you sir. I'm Grant Adams."

"Good to meet you, son." He looked over his shoulder at Evelyn. "If you wouldn't mind, I would like to talk with him in private for a moment."

"As you wish," she said. "I'll tell them to leave you be for the time being."

"I would appreciate that."

Grant watched her go. He had never seen her act so… submissive before. What was going on?

"So I see that your accepted the position that was offered to you," he said to Grant after the door closed.

"I did, Mr. Arno."

"Please, call me Robert, son. Calling me Mr. makes me seem old," he said. "Not that I can deny that charge, mind you, but we can all at least try to keep up our appearances."

"Yes sir."

"Now, you may be wondering why you were selected for something like this, I imagine? Out of thousands of young strapping men, why your name came forward."

Grant frowned. "It crossed my mind, yes."

"And do you know why?"

"Evelyn was very vague," he replied. "She said she had sources."

Robert grunted. "Yes. And she would never want to

accept it, but one of them was myself. Through the appropriate channels, of course."

"I see. May I ask why?"

"Because you have talent, son. I've had my eye on you for quite a while."

That surprised him. "On me?"

"Yes, your success was quite interesting to me. Reminded me of myself in my younger days, in fact. You have talent son, a drive to move forward and take the bull by the horns. I would have recruited you, but there wasn't a good time for it. You would never have left something you had built from the ground up."

Grant nodded. Even with a prestigious offer on the table he would have rather stayed with the company he had helped to create himself. He had invested too much time and effort to simply abandon it. But now...

"Of course, that was before things spiraled out of control for you. I understand what you went through, son. I've had business partners cheat me before in my younger days. Almost put an end to me too. But I fought back, and I learned."

"I'm... still not understanding where this is going."

"You have talent, son. The kind of talent that would be a shame to waste. But you come with a whole lotta baggage, and my group needs to keep its reputation. Even with your exoneration investors aren't going to like you hanging around."

"Not surprising."

"No, but a shame, like I said. You have talent, son, and I'm not going to let someone else scoop that up. You just stay where you are for a few years, build up a bit of credibility and then we can move you up into a real position."

"So this is… me being reserved for something else?" Grant asked warily.

"That's right, son. Keep at it and I can put you back on the path to success."

"I'm flattered, sir." Grant paused for a moment. "Um, does she-"

"Evelyn? No, as far as she's concerned bringing you aboard is completely her idea. I'd like it if it stayed that way."

"Won't she be suspicious because you're talking to me alone?"

"Nothing out of the ordinary, son. I've done the same with her previous assistants. You're just the only one out of them all that's worth a damn."

"I see."

Robert clapped him on the shoulder. "I know it's a lot to take in, son. Just keep moving forward, and you'll be better off in no time. Now, just sit back and enjoy the game. I'm needed down on the field."

Grant stood looking out the window, his mind in turmoil. Was his purpose here just to act as a pawn in everyone else's schemes?

But more importantly, he might have the way out he was looking for. Like he had been told, he just needed to bide his time and wait.

5

Evelyn was almost completely silent on the plane ride back, speaking only when addressed and giving short answers when she did. Grant decided to stay silent for the time being. The sudden mood swing alarmed him even more than it had on the trip to Arlington.

After landing and a short car ride later they were back at Eden Tower. The others headed for their own suites as Grant and Evelyn ascended to their floor.

"Do you need anything else?" he asked when they stepped out of the elevator.

"Yeah. You're coming with me."

Grant couldn't keep the sigh from escaping his lips as she led him toward her suite.

Evelyn glanced back over her shoulder at him. "What?"

"It's nothing."

"Obviously it's something."

"Are you really going to care if I tell you?"

"Probably not."

He had been expecting that, though her bluntness still stung a bit. This was what he had agreed to, though. Grant was well and truly under her thumb, completely at the mercy of her whims, and he had no one to blame but himself.

Just bear it. Just bide his time until he could move on to something better. That was what everyone was expecting, right? That was what *she* was expecting. He was using her, just like she was using him. So why did he feel so conflicted about it?

Maybe it was because he didn't like the feeling of being cornered, where it appeared he had no control over the situation. He knew that wasn't quite true, but it felt like it at the very least.

"Come on," Evelyn said, grabbing his wrist and pulling him through the doorway.

"Do I even have to guess what's going on?"

"No. Now come on."

Grant allowed himself to be pulled along, following her up the stairs and into the loft. She tossed her purse aside into a corner and sat down on the bed, yanking him down beside her.

"Yeah, I thought so."

"See? You didn't even have to guess." She started to pull her jacket off. "Help a little, please."

Grant shrugged off his coat, then undid his tie and dress shirt. As he kicked off his shoes and socks unbuckled his belt Evelyn slipped out of her own attire.

He felt a hand press down into his chest, and an instant later she was on top of him.

"See how easy this goes when you actually help?" Evelyn said.

Grant looked back up at her, feeling her warm, soft skin pressing against his body. She was lovely, stunning, as many men would say, but...

"What is this really about?"

"Hm?"

"Why am I here?"

Evelyn looked down at him. "Why do you think you're here? It seems pretty plain to me, right?"

"No, it doesn't. You're completely silent the whole trip back, you don't say anything to me until we get out on this floor, and then you drag me in here to have sex. That's a pretty big mood swing."

"Huh, it's almost like you're not enjoying this. Am I not good enough for you? I thought I was all those other times."

"That's not it," he protested. "It's..."

"What?"

Grant took a deep breath before he answered. "Is this about your father?"

"What?"

"You're clearly intimidated by him," he said. "Don't deny it. You change when you're around him."

She frowned. "Oh, and even if that's true, what does that have to do with anything?"

"Because you're not in control when you're around him. He has you under his thumb, and you can't do anything to fight back. So am I here just so you can do something to make you feel like you're in control again?"

"What are you, a psychologist now?"

"You're avoiding the question."

"And you're asking ridiculous ones."

Grant decided to press the issue. "It's true, then, isn't it? It's true, but you don't want to admit it, so you're putting up a front. I'm here so you can have someone to dominate."

"Interesting theory," she replied calmly, almost dispassionately, but Grant thought he heard a hint of anger behind her words.

"You're not denying it," he pointed out.

"Whatever." She slid off of him for a second. "Give me your hands."

"Why?"

"Because I said so, OK? Put them over your head."

Grant decided to humor her. "I don't know why you're-"

And then he understood. Grant felt her grasp at his hands, and then something wrapped around his wrists. It felt like soft fabric.

"Is that my tie?"

Evelyn pulled it taut and looped a knot. "Very good."

Grant tried to move his arms, but the knot was far too strong. And in the position she had tied them his palms were against his forearms, making it impossible for him to grab anything or even maneuver his arms. She had him completely at her mercy right now.

"I think this proves my point," he said.

Evelyn gave him a wicked grin. "Maybe I just got this idea from you."

"Yeah, I doubt that."

"Think what you want. You have your own predicament to think about," she said. Grant felt a hand reach between his legs. "What's this? For someone who's protesting so much you body seems to be saying something very different."

"That doesn't mean anything," he protested.

"But your current position does. You let me do this to you."

"Well, now I really can't do anything about it, can I?"

Evelyn shook her head. "Oh, come on, do you really think that one piece of cloth is going to stop you? I have no doubt that if you wanted to you could either break free of that, or you could push me off of you."

Grant didn't respond.

"The question is, will you? I don't think you will," Evelyn said, climbing back on top of him. "For all your complaints about hating being dominated, you certainly seem willing to let me do it."

Grant stayed silent.

"But that's all part of it, isn't it? You're very fair about it, truth be told. You'll use me to get where you want, so you'll let me use you however I wish until the time comes for you to move on. I'm a bit impressed, actually. That's noble in a way."

"How is that noble? That sounds so fucked up when you put it that way."

"But it's true, isn't it? I'm using you, and you're using me. And I think you enjoy the feeling of being dominated."

Grant looked away. "I really don't."

"No need to be bashful. Or maybe that's true, but you seem to be willing to let it happen, at least."

He said nothing in response.

Evelyn wrapped her legs around him. "So let's see about this, OK? I think you'll let me use you any way I see fit. Within reason, of course."

"What are you-" he started to say. He didn't get to finish. Evelyn moved, and a moment later he felt her slide down onto his cock.

"Now, about what you were saying. That I wanted to dominate you, or something like that. Let's play around with that a bit, OK?"

Grant felt her hips start to rock back and forth. "What does that even mean?"

"It means that you're going to lay here and let me do what I want with you. Oh, and you're not allowed to cum until I *let* you."

He didn't have time to respond. Evelyn increased her speed, putting her hands on his shoulders to steady herself. Grant lay still for a moment, then started to thrust back...

And she pulled off of him, a devilish smile on her face.

"Oh come on, really?"

"I didn't say you could do that," she told him.

"You didn't say I couldn't either."

"Ah, then I'll make it a rule. You can only do what I let you do." She slid back on him. "You want to do it. I can feel it. Now, all you need to do is ask, right? Ask me if you can do it."

"Can I do it?" he muttered.

"What? You spoke so quietly that I couldn't hear you."

"Can I do it?"

"Do what?" she teased, the devilish grin still on her face. Grant felt a twinge of anger. Despite her denials of wanting to dominate him she was clearly enjoying this.

He let out a frustrated breath. "Can I fuck you?"

"That didn't sound like it had much conviction behind it. I wouldn't want to force you to spend all this energy on something you didn't enjoy." She leaned down over him with a smile on her face. "Unless you want to ask again?"

"Are you serious?"

"Mmm, and aren't you in a bind here? Literally, in fact. You can't even satisfy your urges unless I let you, and you're not making a very good case for yourself. So, do you care to ask again?"

"Can I fuck you?"

"Oh? That almost sounds more like a demand than a request."

"Are you kidding?"

"Maybe you should ask the right question, hm?

Remember who's in control here."

Grant went silent for a moment, trying to figure out what she was talking about. This was all just a game to her, and right now he was simply playing along. The thought frustrated him.

He looked up at her. "Will you let me fuck you?"

She smiled. "There you go. Yes, I think I'll let you."

Evelyn began rocking her hips back and forth, pressing down on his chest this time. Grant thrust back, pushing forward with his frustration and need for release. He could hear her beginning to breath hard, felt his own chest heaving. He felt it building inside of him…

And then she pushed back off again.

"Seriously, what the hell?" he said angrily.

"Aw, is someone upset that their fun was interrupted?" Evelyn taunted him. "You didn't ask."

"Are we really going back to this again?"

"You didn't ask. Now, what do you want to do?"

Grant tried not to show his frustration. "Will you let me cum?"

Evelyn climbed back on top of him and looked down, the wicked grin back on her face. "I will. When *I* decide to let you."

They went back and forth for a while before Evelyn finally granted him release. How long had it been? A half hour? An hour? Maybe even longer? Grant had no idea. He wasn't in a particularly good mood, either. Evelyn had granted him release, but little satisfaction came with it. She had thoroughly dominated him, stripping him of all control and dignity in the process.

She reached up to his arms and undid the knot, climbing off of him and allowing him to sit up. Grant rubbed his wrists for a moment before he stood up and moved to gather his clothing.

"You're not done yet," she told him.

"What else is there to do? Don't tell me that you want to go again."

Evelyn stood up as well. "No. But I feel dirty from spending all that time around my father. I'm going to take a shower."

"OK?"

"You're coming with me."

Grant sighed. "Fine."

"Don't look so unhappy about it."

He followed her into the bathroom and stepped into the shower with her. It was large, probably big enough to fit a half-dozen people it without trouble. Evelyn turned the handles, and a moment later hot water began to cascade down over their bodies.

"Is this it?"

She gave him a look. "What do you mean, is this it?"

"If you're just going to take a shower then why do you need me here?"

"Maybe I wanted some company?"

"Yeah, I'm sure that's it," Grant replied sarcastically.

"There's always something going on with you."

"Or maybe you're just thinking about it too much," Evelyn said. "You can't even relax when you're given the chance."

"I'm a lot better off than you are."

"Oh?"

Grant scowled. "Don't tell me you just did all of that for your amusement. If that's true then why didn't you do anything like that before?"

"I have my reasons."

"Yeah, I'm sure. The one day it happens is the one day you have to see your father and completely lose it."

"Like you'd know anything about that."

"I probably know a lot more about it than you," he replied.

"Whatever. Come here and wash me," she ordered.

"What?"

"Come here and wash me off," Evelyn repeated.

Grant hesitated for a moment.

"Was I not clear?" she said pointedly.

Her last statement made something inside of him snap. Grant moved over to Evelyn and spun her around.

"What are-" she started to say.

Grant slammed a hand into the side of the shower, trapping her against the wall with his own body. Evelyn's eyes widened for a moment.

"What the hell?" he demanded. "Am I just here so you can work out your issues with your father? So you can dominate a man when you know you're completely under the thumb of another?"

"That's-"

"What the hell? *What the hell?*" he repeated, feeling the anger rising inside of him. "Why did you drag me into this? Do you really hate your father that much?"

"Yes. Why wouldn't I feel this way? I'm not a daughter to him, I'm just a pawn in his schemes."

That was definitely true in light of what Grant had been told, but...

But the anger still had too firm of a grip on him.

"And that's enough that you're willing to use me as a pawn too, is that right? You have a lot more in common with your dad than you think."

She looked him in the eye with a cold glare. "You don't know a damn thing."

"Neither do you. You think you hate your father? You don't know the first thing about that. You're just disdainful about him, nothing more."

"And what the hell would you know about it?" she demanded.

Grant clenched a fist. "Ever been beaten so badly by your father that you couldn't even sit or lie down without hurting yourself even more? Ever hide under your covers at night trying not to hear what he's doing to your mom? Ever see him hit your mother so hard in a fit of rage that she goes into a coma and never wakes up?"

He suddenly realized that he had pressed Evelyn up

against the shower wall and stepped back.

"I'm sorry," he muttered, not daring to look her in the eye.

"It's fine. You can go now," she said abruptly.

Grant hesitated for a moment.

"Just go."

He stepped out of the shower and grabbed a towel to dry off. As Grant left the bathroom he heard the sound of a sigh, barely audible over the noise of the shower.

"Damn you," he heard Evelyn say.

6

Grant tried to break the ice the next morning.

"Look," he said to Evelyn at breakfast the next morning, "I'm sorry about-"

"Don't be," she interrupted him. "I'm not mad at you."

"Are you just saying that?"

"Of course not. If I wasn't happy with you then you'd know. It's fine."

Grant wasn't exactly convinced, but he decided to leave it at that for the time being.

"Alright then. What are you planning on doing today?" he asked.

"Nothing. Yesterday took a lot out of me, so I'm not going to do much today. You're lucky that I'm even out of bed at this point."

Grant shook his head. "Really?"

"Yes, really. You're pretty much free for the rest of the

day. What are you planning on doing?"

He took a bite of egg and chewed, thinking. "I'm not sure. I think that I might watch the markets today."

"Can't let it go, huh?"

"I've spent most of my adult life in finance, so of course I'm not going to just let it go. And I want to stay in practice," he said.

Grant may have been offered a position within the Arno Group at a later date, but he didn't think for a second that the offer would stay on the table if he proved to be incompetent. He had to keep his skills sharp, and the only way to do that was through practice and observation.

Plus, now that he had a reasonably steady paycheck it was a good idea to invest some of it.

"Do you have what you need?"

"I have my laptop. That should be enough for my purposes."

She scoffed. "Just a laptop? Is that all you're using?"

"Like I said, it's fine for my purposes."

"You need to think bigger. Like, a whole lot bigger," Evelyn told him. "How much of your suit do you actually use?"

"So far? The bedroom, bathroom and occasionally the study and living room."

"And there's several more rooms in there. You could easily have one configured into a day trading room. Or maybe more, if you like."

"More than one? What kind of monstrosity are you

thinking about?"

"I don't know, something with more screens, more processing power. You'd be the best judge of that."

"I'm fine as it is, thank you," Grant replied. "I'm not doing day trading right now, so there's no point in me throwing that much money into it."

"Suit yourself," she said. "But if you want..."

"I don't have infinite funds to throw away."

"Huh, you may not, but you're not the only one here, are you? Maybe if you did a little bit of convincing..."

Grant shook his head. "Thank you for the offer, but I really don't want to be any more indebted to you than I already am. And I'm not sure I want to know what your idea of convincing is."

"Tch, you complain so much about it and yet when the time comes you can't actually resist," Evelyn commented. "I'm starting to think that you might actually like being dominated."

"I'd say that there's evidence to the contrary, and leave it that," Grant replied, thinking about the previous night.

"Maybe. Or maybe you like the seesaw. The back and forth."

"Can we talk about something else?"

"What about?"

"Yesterday was the first time I saw you interact with your sisters," he said. "I know that you might not exactly be fond of them..."

"I don't hate them. I just don't get them," Evelyn told

him.

"Not exactly sure what you mean by that either."

Evelyn took a bite and chewed for a moment. "I don't exactly get living your whole life inside a tower without a care in the world. I don't get just being a bystander to everything."

"But aren't you doing the same thing?"

"Yes, I am. Not by choice, though."

"What's holding you back?"

"My father."

The answer didn't surprise him. "That seems to be the answer to everything wrong in your life, isn't it?"

"Probably because it's true. Especially in this case. What else am I going to do?"

"Aren't you involved in the Arno Corporation?"

"Once again, just like everything else it's just window dressing. I have no power to enact or do anything, and that's not going to change any time soon."

"And your father is the cause of this?"

"He's the head of the corporation, so yes, this is his doing."

Grant took another bite. "That's... not really the impression I got of him. He seemed to be the pragmatic type."

"Oh, did he pull the routine on you?" Evelyn asked. Grant could hear annoyance in her voice.

"Routine?"

"Oh, he's very nice and charming, yes? He's like that to

all males. Put him with a woman and it's an entirely different story."

"How does he manage to last in the business world acting that way?"

"Money cures a lot of ills. And he can turn up the charm when he needs to as well. Don't let that fool you, though. He's as black-hearted as they come, and he'll use you as a chess piece in the blink of an eye."

"I see."

"And don't tell me that I'm like him. Might look like it on the surface, but there's a difference."

"I couldn't tell."

"That's enough out of you."

"Well, why don't you enlighten me as to the difference."

She looked at him. "The difference is that he simply does whatever he wants. I ask for permission first."

Grant wondered about that. He wondered if she actually believed what she was saying, or whether it was just something she was repeating to distance herself from her father. He wondered whether she even considered the force and implied threats she used to get her way. Evelyn clearly had leverage over him, and Grant wasn't exactly in a position to refuse. He had the *option* to refuse, but taking it would only lead to more trouble.

He wondered why she was even bothering to justify herself in front of him. At this point Grant was completely under her thumb whether he was willing or not.

But he remembered their confrontation the previous

night and said nothing, not wishing to provoke her again.

She continued speaking, apparently oblivious to his inner thoughts. "Anyhow, I'm not doing anything today, so you're free for whatever."

"Staying trapped in the tower?"

"You can leave whenever you want. You're not bound here like some of the rest of us."

"I wouldn't quite say that..."

She gave him a coy smile. "Oh, still can't resist, huh?"

"That's not what I meant."

Evelyn laughed. "You're too easy."

Grant shook his head. "Sometimes I don't get you."

"That's fair. I don't exactly get you either."

He leaned back in his chair. "I don't get it. You seem like you're dead set against being caged up in here, yet you don't seem to be doing anything about it. I don't get that."

"I have my reasons."

"As always," Grant finished. "But do they mean anything?"

Surprisingly, she didn't deflect the question.

"I guess it's just a part of how I grew up and what I know. You said something last night about your own father?"

Grant winced. "Yeah, I did."

"I won't talk about it if you don't want."

"No, it's fine. It's in the past, and I've come to terms with what happened. What about it?"

"Why did you never do anything to try to stop what

was happening?"

"I was pretty young at that point," he said.

"But you mother never thought about escaping?"

"I think she was too afraid," Grant said. "Looking back... Looking back I wish I was able to do something. Anything. Anything I could do to keep it from happening."

"What would you have done?"

"Honestly?" he said, looking her in the eye. "I wish I had killed him. Even right after it happened I felt that way."

"How old were you?"

"About ten."

Evelyn frowned. "Well, I can't say I blame you. But I guess it might make you understand?"

"How so?"

"Leaving... trying to change anything is hard. It's sometimes easier to just leave things the way they are and hope they'll get better in the future."

"But if they don't?"

"Then it's not good in situations like yours. But I can't really compare myself to that. I'm luckier than most. I'm provided for, I have a home. I'm not starving, I'm not in danger of being beaten or raped, I have a certain amount of freedom. Compared to most I can't complain."

"Even so," Grant said, then paused for a moment. "Even so, is that enough?"

He saw a smile cross Evelyn's face, softer, sadder than anything he had seen from her before. For a fleeting moment he felt nothing but pity for her.

"I think I'll manage," she told him, and then the smile was gone. The one that replaced it was colder, harder.

"I'm sure you will," Grant said.

She nodded. "I'm here, and I'm fine with that. Other than those times I have to see my father I don't have anything to complain about."

"I understand. I think."

Evelyn laughed. "That's good. I'd like to keep a little mystery going on around you."

And just like that, the games had begun once again.

The call came out of the blue. Grant was in the middle of reading a book when his cell phone started vibrating on the table beside his chair. He quickly marked his spot and picked it up.

Brody.

"Hello?"

"Hi Grant, it's me."

"You picked an odd time to call," Grant said, looking at the clock. "An afternoon on a Monday?"

"I have the day off today. If this isn't a good time then I can call back later."

"Oh no, I wasn't doing anything. Actually, I was given the day off today as well."

"Lucky. Barely there over a week and you get a day off," Brody said.

"Well, I did have to work yesterday. And work can be hit or miss. It depends on what my boss wants me to do that day."

"How are you liking it?"

Grant hesitated for a moment, wondering how to respond. What was he supposed to say, that he was stuck here as the boy toy to an Arno Corporation heiress? Or even worse, that he hadn't taken the chance to back away when it had been offered to him?

"There have been ups and downs," he said, choosing his words carefully. "My boss can be demanding sometimes, and a lot of it is menial tasks."

And not so menial tasks, he thought to himself.

"But you do have your foot in the door," Brody said. "And knowing you you'll be able to work your way up the ladder. Pretty soon you'll be meeting with the head honchos."

"I actually already met Robert Arno yesterday."

"Oh? How was that?"

"I think it went well," Grant said.

"That's good to hear."

"How have Jayden and Cole been?"

"Bundles of energy, as always. They both want to know when Uncle Grant is coming to visit. Jayden especially."

Grant smiled. "Unfortunately I really can't give them a good answer for that. I'd love to, but with the way things are going right now I'm not sure that I'd be able to get the time off."

"That's fine. After what you've been through you need to take the time to get back up on your feet. Do whatever it takes to make that happen."

If only he knew what that actually meant.

"I'll try to see if I can make it happen. It's been too long since I've seen you guys."

"Well, if you can make it happen that's great, but like I said, don't put too much pressure on yourself. Getting back on your feet is your top priority."

"That's going to take some doing."

"No doubt that you'll be able to do it, bro."

"Thanks for the vote of confidence."

"Don't mention it. I've seen how you work, and I believe in you."

"Thanks."

"Well, I'll let you go now. Good luck."

"Thanks. Give Sonya and the boys my love."

"Will do."

Grant set down his phone and leaned back in his chair, looking up at the ceiling. Thoughts started swirling through his mind. He might not be where he imagined, but...

But at least he had someone he could rely upon. Even through all the rough years and terror growing up he could rely on Brody, and the same was true in reverse. No matter what happened they would be there to support each other.

Evelyn, though...

For a moment he felt a twinge of sympathy for her. Three siblings, and yet she seemed distant from all of them. Despite her demeanor, despite her insistence that she was fine in her current position, Grant couldn't help feeling that she was lonely. Facing too many challenges alone could be terrifying.

Maybe that was why he was here. For all her bluster and the fronts she was putting up, Evelyn might be nothing more than a loner looking for a companion to stand beside her.

That might explain her behavior, but it didn't make him feel much better. She was still toying with him, using him for her own purposes. Could he really do anything to stop that?

Or should he even bother? She had said it herself, this was only a stepping stone to something better for him. If she wasn't content, Evelyn was at least accepting of her fate. Was this really his problem? He wanted to ignore it all, wanted to just let it all fade into the background, but...

"Why couldn't this be normal?" he muttered to himself.

That was all he wanted. Some normal way to rebuild his life and get back on his feet. Just an opportunity to set things right. Why couldn't he get it? Why was he being forced to play this ridiculous game to get where he needed to be?

And why was he even bothering to stick around for all of this? There had to be some better way to accomplish what he wanted, something that would let his dignity stay intact. Yet he was still here.

Maybe she was right. Maybe he secretly liked the idea of being dominated.

Grant pushed that thought aside angrily. He had spent more than enough of his life dominated, being at the mercy of someone he couldn't even fight back against. Why would that be any different now?

He wanted to deny it. He wanted to push it all away and forget it all. But the thought wouldn't leave him.

Z

The next few days passed without incident. Evelyn made few demands of him, and Grant was content to settle into a routine. Other than accompanying her to meals and spending a few hours with her each day there was no degree of difficulty. Most of her teasing had stopped as well.

Grant appreciated the change, but he wondered if something was amiss. She had seemed different over the past few days, subdued, distant. It was a far cry from the forceful, headstrong woman that had come into his life. Was it something he had said, or were there other factors completely out of his control at play?

He didn't have much time to ponder it. A text message interrupted his thoughts. As expected, it was from Evelyn.

Come to my room.

"What now?" he mumbled to himself, standing up out of his chair and heading out of his suite.

Grant had expected to be done for the day, especially since it was ten at night. What could she want at a time like this, especially when she seemed to be showing a lot of restraint lately? Was that about to change.

Evelyn was outside her doorway when he arrived.

"What's up?" Grant asked.

"We have somewhere to go."

"Now?"

"We're not leaving the building," she said, motioning for him to follow. Evelyn headed in the direction of the elevators.

"Where are we going?"

"The top floor of the tower, to the penthouse."

"To do..."

"Well, apparently there's a party up there," she said. "Apparently my sisters decided to throw yet another booze and drug fest, apparently it's happening tonight, and apparently I need to be there."

"Couldn't you refuse?"

"Then I get accused of being unsociable. Most of the guests come from powerful business families, so there's that. According to my father we're supposed to be friendly with them."

"And that includes getting drugged out of your mind?"

"*Tch*. As if. I'm going up there, putting in my appearance and leaving."

"So why do I have to go along?"

"Because someone else has to suffer with me," she said

as she pressed the elevator button.

"Gee, thanks a lot."

"It won't take that long."

"You could just not go," he suggested, stepping into the elevator with her.

"On the off chance that Rosalie and Josephine aren't completely smashed, I'll never hear the end of it. And even if they are hammered someone might mention that they didn't see me there, and that's just going to cause trouble."

Grant leaned up against the side of the elevator. "So you're just going along with it, going to something you hate just to avoid making waves?"

"I don't want to be disturbed, that's all. I'll do this on my own terms."

"Can you really call it your own terms when you're being coerced into it?"

"I made the final choice," she replied, then changed the subject. "Rule of thumb. Don't drink anything, don't eat anything, unless you want to be as high as a kite. Unless you're really into that kind of thing."

"I've done more than enough of that in college to last a lifetime, so I'm good."

"Good. We're probably going to be there for only a few minutes or so. Don't get too caught up in what's happening. Oh, and don't get into any fights. Try to stay with me too."

Grant gave her a look. "This is sounding like we're going to the worst nightclub ever."

"That's a pretty good description of it, actually. I think

I'll use that in the future."

"I noticed that you didn't say anything about Miranda."

"She's not going to be there. Never is."

"So why can she get away with it and you can't?"

"Because that's expected of her. She's the introvert with no social life and no friends that hides in her room all the time."

"Does she have a million cats?"

"Just one."

"Still fits the description."

Grant saw her smile slightly. "Just a little," she commented.

And then there was no more time to talk. The elevator doors opened, and Grant heard the sound of pulsating musing up ahead. He followed Evelyn down the hallway and through one of the doors at the end.

Immediately his senses were overwhelmed, bombarded by a myriad of sights, sounds, smells. Music boomed throughout the penthouse, almost drowning out the buzz of conversation. The area sat bathed in a purple light, and he could see smoke wafting around some areas. Grant was pretty sure it wasn't from cigarettes.

"Evie, so you did show up!"

Grant saw a trio of young women pick their way through the crowd, drinks in hand. Two looked like they were identical twins with red hair, and the other had her black hair made up into a bun.

"Hello," Evelyn said, giving them an unenthusiastic

wave.

In the blink of an eye they had her surrounded.

"You're late."

"You've missed so much. Donny's here, and so is Hugh. You should really see them."

Evelyn tried to back up a bit. "Well, I wouldn't want to-"

One of them grabbed her by the arm. "Oh come on, you should totally talk to him. Are you too shy for it?"

Grant stood frozen for a moment, unsure of what exactly was happening in front of him. Before he could react the others had disappeared into the crowd, Evelyn in tow.

Now what?

He moved deeper into the penthouse, trying to catch a glimpse of her. If he could figure out some sort of excuse to get her away from the others…

Or maybe he should just leave her here. It would serve her right, having to be at the beck and call of someone else. Some might call it karma.

Grant shook his head. No, he couldn't leave her here. He at least needed to make some sort of effort to find her.

Chaos and hedonism unfolded all around him as he walked through the penthouse. Alcohol flowed freely, and he caught a glimpse of white powder being spread in lines across a table.

Someone reached out and grabbed him by the wrist.

"You look like you're lost," a female voice said.

Grant turned around to see a young woman looking

back at him, scantily clad and likely drunk.

"You look like you need something to do," she said.

"I'm fine, thank-"

She put a finger on his lips. "Oh, you're a pretty one. Maybe you want to come with me?"

"Um..." Grant began to protest, just as she began to pull him in down one of the other hallways.

"You need to have some fun, pretty boy. Come on."

She pulled him down the hallway and into a side room.

Grant had expected it to be empty, but it wasn't. Several people were already present, all of them naked. He suddenly realized that he had been pulled right into the middle of an orgy.

Grant tried to step away, but his captor kept a tight grip on his wrist.

"What's the matter? Sit down and have a little bit of fun."

She pushed him onto a couch and a moment later straddled him. He felt her hands starting to fumble around with his pants, wondering how he should respond. He had been told not to offend anyone, but...

And then the girl slipped off. Grant sat up, confused. Had she passed out?

No, he realized, she hadn't. Someone had redirected her and was standing before him.

"That's not... It's not what it looks like," he said.

Evelyn had an icy edge to her glare. She grabbed his wrist and pulled him up, then led him out of the room and through the mess in the main penthouse. A short while later they were back in the elevator.

"Couldn't resist, huh?" she said.

"That's wasn't my fault," he protested. "I tried to come look for you, but then she sidetracked me, and then-"

"And then you end up in there, is that right?"

"I told you, I didn't go in there by choice. What's it to you anyhow?"

She didn't respond.

"So is this it for tonight?" he asked.

"No. You're coming with me."

Evelyn grabbed him by the wrist as the elevator doors opened and pulled him toward her suite. Once inside she led him up to the loft.

"Now, here's somewhere a little more peaceful," Evelyn said, sitting down on the bed. She reached up to pull him down beside her.

Grant swatted her hand aside, and a look of confusion briefly crossed her face.

"What are you-"

"What the hell is wrong with you?" he demanded angrily. "I told you that wasn't my fault, and yet you throw a fit and take it out on me. I wouldn't have even been in that position if you didn't drag me up there. And yet you're pissed about it?"

"When did I tell you that screwing random people up there is OK?"

Grant took a deep breath and exhaled, trying to keep

his anger in check.

"I don't get you. I just don't. Why are you so upset about this? Are you pissed off because the thing you thought belonged to you and you only was going to get taken by someone else? Are you that alone and lonely that you have to hoard me so no one else can try to take me?"

"That's not-"

"I think it is. I think you're using me, and I think you don't like it when someone comes in and destroys your perfect little world where you're queen and everyone is under your foot."

"That's interesting. And what makes you think something so ridiculous?"

"You drag me into this every time. Every time something happens where you're not in control you drag me in here to try to dominate me. You're doing it so you can feel better about having no control over your life, right? Don't deny it."

"That's interesting, coming from someone who's a masochist and likes being dominated himself."

"Hardly."

He saw a vicious smile cross her face.

"Oh really? Let's look at this closer, shall we? You say I'm using you? Who's the one living here on my dime, using this as a way to get back into good standing so he can use it to further his career, hm? Who's really using who here?"

"That's not-"

"Oh, and another thing, cut the sanctimonious bullshit

about being forced into having sex with me. I've given you *plenty* of chances to say no, and you haven't taken one. You enjoy it and then have the gall to complain so you can make yourself into a martyr."

"That's not-"

"Oh, but it is. You seem to want to deny it, but when you get right down to the heart of it you secretly like it, don't you? It's everything you wanted, only you don't want to openly admit it. So you play the part of the wounded deer while continuing to go along with it."

He looked away. "Yeah yeah, men are dogs. I get it."

"A dog? Don't flatter yourself. You come when called, you do all the tricks when ordered, but you're no dog. A dog has teeth. A dog can snap back when it's cornered. When have you ever shown the ability to do that?"

"Shut up."

Evelyn leaned forward. "No, you're not a dog. Not even close. You're just a *puppy*."

Grant felt the anger boil up inside of him and whirled around.

"I didn't say that you could leave. Now come here."

He stopped in his tracks and hesitated, still seething from her biting comments. She was so wrong, and yet…

And yet…

Grant felt a hand grab his wrist and pull him back. He let himself be dragged along, back from the stairs and toward the bed.

Evelyn pushed him down on his back. "And there you

go. You're so well trained."

He scowled at her.

"Tell you what, I'll give you another choice," she said as she started to strip off his clothing. "You'll have the opportunity to walk away from this right now. You can go back to your room and spend the night jerking off, or whatever."

Grant let her pull off his shirt and said nothing.

"Or, you can stay here and enjoy yourself. That's not so bad, is it?"

She pulled off his pants, then shed her own clothes.

"So what will it be?"

Grant didn't move.

"I'll take that as a yes, then."

He let out a long sigh. "You really have a way of making me feel like a fool."

"Is that such a bad thing? Who's the one that's determining that you're a fool or not, the rest of the world? The rest of the world is insane."

Grant felt her breasts press into his chest as she leaned down.

"Face it, no matter how much to protest about it, the truth of the matter is that you want me."

"I'll admit that you're hard to resist," he said.

"*Tch*, still trying to play it cool, I see. Well fine. We can make it more fun that way."

"Is this really how it's going to be? Is this all there is?"

"What do you want it to be?"

Grant didn't answer for a moment. "I don't know," he said. "But is this what it should be?"

"Oh, so you're a romantic, is that it?" Evelyn said with another coy smile. "Thinking that you're in some fairy tale. It's set up perfectly, isn't it?"

"How so?"

Evelyn moved and straddled him, wrapping her legs around him and putting her hands on his shoulders.

"It's the perfect fairy tale. I'm the princess trapped in the tower, held captive by the evil lord and her wicked sisters, and you're the white knight that gets to ride in to the rescue."

"That really never crossed my mind," he replied.

"Oh really? Then why are you still here, obeying my every command?"

"I have my reasons."

She smiled. "Stealing my catchphrase. Not a way to endear yourself to me."

"What, was pushing you into the shower wall not alluring enough?"

That made her laugh. "I'll admit, that surprised me. And I'll admit that I might have gone too far. But I'm glad I did. You actually showed a bit of spine there."

"And yet you're still taunting me about not being able to resist you," he said. "What is it?"

"Oh, you have a spine," Evelyn replied, leaning down close to him. "But I have control over you. That's what makes it so interesting."

"What, did everyone else not meet your standards?"

"It's no fun if you just go along with what I want."

"So you're provoking me on purpose, is that it?" Grant asked. "Why, so you can feel powerful when you can dominate a man that's resisting? Are your daddy issues that bad?"

"Don't talk about my father in bed. That's the fastest way to kill the mood," Evelyn replied.

"I think the mood's already dead for me."

"Your mouth says that, but the rest of your body speaks very differently," she said, reaching a hand down between her legs. "Rock hard." Evelyn grinned impishly. "So much for not being in the mood."

"It's involuntary," Grant protested.

Evelyn laughed and rolled off of him. "Oh yes, it is. But you still can't deny how turned on you are."

Grant sat up as she crawled to the middle of the bed and stood up on her knees.

"Are you just going to keep teasing me?"

"Aw, do you need some release?" she replied. "I'll tell you what, you can be dominant this time."

She leaned forward on all fours and looked back at him.

"Think you can handle this? *Puppy*," she said tauntingly.

Grant scowled. "As if."

The next thing he knew he was behind her and had his arms wrapped around her waist. One thrust later and he was inside.

"Ahhh. Ah, so you do have it in you," she said.

"So do you."

"Mmph. I should kick you out of bed for making such a terrible pun, but I won't."

Everything else seemed to fade away. The heat of her body, the softness of her skin, the wetness between her legs, those were the only things he could sense right now.

And right in the moment, nothing else mattered.

Sunlight streamed through the windows, and Grant began to slowly wake up. In the chaos of last night he had forgotten to put the shades down. He rubbed the sleep from his eyes and began to move, looking for the clock so he could check the time.

But then he bumped something with one of his hands, and Grant realized he wasn't in his own bed. He heard the sound of someone else moving and opened his eyes in time to see Evelyn wake up.

"Wait, I'm still here?" he said.

"What the heck does that mean?" Evelyn said sleepily.

"I could have sworn that I left..."

"Mmm, maybe you dreamed about it," she said, sitting up. She was still naked.

"Maybe?"

"But you crashed pretty hard last night after all the fireworks. There was no sense in making you get up and go back to your own room, so..."

Grant thought for a moment. "Yeah, we did get pretty wild last night, didn't we?"

"I think maybe I'll start provoking you during sex more. You fuck better when you're angry," she grinned at him.

"Whatever."

"You know, you say that you don't get me, but you're quite the mystery yourself."

"Huh?"

"Oh, think about it for a second. You're a bundle of contradictions. You're here to salvage your reputation, right? To get back on your feet so you can go back to your old life and status. Isn't that right?"

Grant didn't respond.

"No need to be ashamed about it. That was part of the agreement, right? But that's where things start to get very interesting, hm?"

"Interesting?"

She looked down at him. "I think I know what you're doing, actually. You claim that you're being pushed into following my orders. That I'm just dominating you. And maybe you're right. But maybe there's more to it."

"OK?"

"I think you're rationalizing. You might have come here to get your old life back, but then you suddenly started to realize you liked it here, and that derails all your plans."

Grant shook his head. "Oh. So this is all just wild speculation."

"There you go again trying to play it cool, but you really can't deny it, can you? You're just going along with everything I tell you. If you really hated it then you'd dig in your heels and refuse at some point, right? I've given you plenty of opportunities. But you haven't done that."

"Can you really say I have an opportunity when you have the threat of cutting me lose to hang over my head? That's really not much of a choice."

"I'm not going to do that just because you refused me a few times. And you can always be moved somewhere else to salvage your reputation. But you don't want that, do you? You want to stay here."

Grant couldn't think of a retort.

"Maybe you weren't like that at the beginning, but that changed. You can deny it, but deep down you know it's true. You want me, and that's why you can't resist me."

"Believe what you want."

"Oh, I think it's far past the point of believing things. I know that's going through your mind, whether you want to admit it or not. And as much as you might not like it, you secretly want it that way, don't you?"

Grant shook his head and started rise, but Evelyn pushed him back down.

"I'm just-"

"I didn't say that you could get back up," she said with a devilish smile, straddling him again. "You got to be on top every time last night, so it's only fair that you return the favor, right?"

"And we're just going to forget all the other times?"

"None of those count. Protest all you want. You know that you're not actually going to fight back."

She pushed the covers back, revealing the full splendor of her naked body in the morning light. And once again, he couldn't resist her.

8

The cat wouldn't leave him alone.

It had looked at Grant curiously when he sat down, its green eyes staring at him in vivid contrast to its black coat. Grant had absentmindedly reached out and stroked it on the back of the head, thinking nothing of it in the moment, but now the cat was on his lap. Every time he stopped stroking it stood up and meowed at him.

"He likes you," Miranda commented with a smile.

"Yeah, I noticed. Is he like that with everyone?"

"Some he is, some he isn't. I think Midnight wants attention from you because you're new, and he's making sure that you notice him."

"Huh, sounds a lot like someone else," Grant commented.

"Wonder who that could be," Evelyn said dryly.

"Oh, I'll think of a name eventually," he quipped back.

Miranda giggled. "Oh, squabbles?"

"Nothing out of the ordinary," Evelyn said. "Nothing like Rose or Josie's drama."

Grant wondered exactly what kind of drama she considered more extreme than their own, but said nothing.

Instead he glanced around Miranda's suite, trying to get some sense of who she was from her surroundings. Even after only meeting her for a short while Grant got the impression that she was far different from the rest of her siblings. While Rosalie and Josephine were firmly entrenched in their hedonist lifestyle, and Evelyn went along with a barely disguised contempt for it, Miranda seemed to be above it all.

In fact, she seemed to be in her own little world. Her suite had none of the flair or aesthetics of some of the others he had seen. In fact, most of the walls were either covered with bookshelves or areas for a cat to climb through and hang around.

"I notice that you have a lot of books," Grant commented. "I'm guessing that you're a reader?"

"That's a safe bet," she said.

"How many books do you have? I've seen libraries with smaller collections."

"Honestly, I've lost count. It's probably in the tens of thousands at this point."

"And you've read all of them?"

"Yes. I'm a fast reader, and I spend a lot of my time doing it."

"You would think-"

He looked down as the cat butted its head into his chest and realized he had stopped petting it. Grant ran his hand down its back, groaning inside. His comment about it being like Evelyn was becoming more and more apt by the second. Both of them kept demanding his attention.

"Wouldn't an e-reader be a better way to store things? It must be hard trying to find a book you want."

"I'm honestly surprised you haven't tried to catalogue them all," Evelyn said.

"That would take a lot of time."

"Well, you could hire someone to do it. God knows that it would make finding things a lot simpler."

Miranda looked at him. "To answer your question, I don't like e-readers."

"Oh?"

"They're so soulless. They don't have the character, the feel of a paper book. They just lack something solid. Am I making sense?"

"No, it makes sense. I've heard it put that way before," Grant said. "I always thought that it was the words that gave the book its character, no matter what it was written on."

Miranda smiled. "Put that way, I can't really argue with that. So I guess it comes down to a personal preference of mine. I just like paper books."

"That I can understand."

"I think you picked a good personal assistant this time," she said to Evelyn.

"Thanks, I try."

"Is there any reason why you don't have one? A personal assistant, I mean," Grant asked.

"I have no need for one. I don't do the things that Rose or Josie do. Or Evie, for that matter, so there's no reason for me to have one."

"I see," Grant replied, trying to dance around the issue. He was almost sorry that he asked.

"You should really get out more," Evelyn said.

"So now you're stepping into Josie and Rose's shoes?" Miranda asked with a smile. "Trying to get me to be normal, whatever that means?"

"That's not what I meant. I don't mean that you have to turn into one of them, but you almost never leave the tower unless you have to."

"I like it here," she shrugged. "Why leave when I don't have to?"

"Because there's things outside that you might be missing? Why don't you come with us one of the times when we go out?" Evelyn offered.

"Thank you, but I'm content where I am. And I'm not going to change that just to meet an expectation."

"I thought so, but I thought I needed to make the offer regardless."

"Oh, I know. And I know you're asking out of kindness. But really, I'm fine," Miranda said.

"Now, if only the other two could take some cues from you," Evelyn said.

"They have their own way of doing things, and I won't begrudge them for that."

"Yeah. You didn't have to be their little doll growing up."

Grant saw Miranda look back at him. "You must be completely confused about this whole thing."

"I am-"

The cat pressed its head into his chest again as he stopped petting it. That was more than enough for now. Grant picked him up and placed him right on Evelyn's lap.

"Gosh, thanks," she said, giving him a withering look as the cat turned his attention to her instead.

"Don't mention it." He looked back at Miranda. "To be honest, I'm a little confused about how everything happens here. It seems... disconnected. Like, you're all sort of living under the same roof..."

"But yet we all seem like strangers?"

"That's not quite how I'd put it." He thought for a moment. "I guess it seems more like the relationship I have with my brother. Only, we live hundreds of miles apart, so we can't see each other often."

"So we seem distant from each other?"

"Sort of? Like, it's almost like there's a physical distance between everyone even though you're all living in the same building."

"Like we have walls around us that separate us. More of the metaphoric kind, not the physical."

"Yes, sort of like that."

"Well, there's the age distance. And then there's the difference between the way that we all chose to live our lives," Miranda explained. "That alone seems to create a great distance between us."

"Believe me, you're not the only one that feels that way," Evelyn spoke up. "Sometimes I wish I could be like you and not care what they think of me going against their lifestyle."

"They're doing what they think is best."

"*Tch*. Then they're pretty lacking in judgement, which isn't a very big surprise."

"Nice to know that you have such a high opinion about your sisters," Grant commented.

"You saw what goes on. What makes you think I want anything to have to do with something like that?"

Grant shrugged and said nothing. In truth, he couldn't exactly see much difference between her actions and that of her sisters. It was simply a matter of scale.

"You two seem to get along pretty well," he said. "Or at least better than you do with the other two."

He saw Miranda smile.

"Well, it's really not that unusual," Evelyn spoke up. "We're closer in age. And both of are are the oddballs of the family, so it's only natural that we'd gravitate toward each other."

"I'm an oddball, Evie. You definitely aren't," Miranda told her.

"I'd beg to differ on that. I'm nothing like any of the

others, and both of us are treated differently as well."

"Are you talking about dad?"

"I guess," she said. Grant noticed her frown slightly.

"I think that's because he expects more out of you than from Rose and Josie. And me."

"If he does, he doesn't show it very well. I'm just another wallflower he has to provide for, and that's it. I was born with the wrong parts."

"I think you're being a little too hard on yourself."

"I don't think so. I think that it would have been much easier if one of us had been born a boy," Evelyn said. "He'd have his heir to carry on his legacy. But instead he got stuck with four goals, and they're not good enough to hack it in the business world."

"I've known plenty of women who were a lot better than me in that world," Grant said.

"Of course you did. You're not stuck living in the fifties where every woman is chained to the stove in the kitchen," she said unhappily. "If given the choice he'd definitely favor you."

Grant didn't mention how true those words might be. That part needed to stay silent for the time being. At this point he wasn't even sure he'd take it, especially after their previous spat. Being called out about using her for his own personal gain had cut him more than he thought it would. Evelyn might be doing the same thing, but...

But even so, it touched something deep inside of him. Some might say he was justified returning the favor, using her as she used him, but that didn't sit well with Grant. He had made a vow long ago to be better than his father, to not carry his burdens or his sins. He'd grow beyond that.

And that made the prospect of using Evelyn as merely a stepping stone a very touchy subject in his mind, one he wasn't sure he wanted to take. The fact that the offer had come from her father made it even worse in his mind, and Evelyn would probably flip out if she ever discovered that.

"So you two bonded because you're both outsiders in your family? Because you can relate to each other?"

"That about sums it up," Miranda confirmed. "And we have our differences, but we don't let that divide us. We're very different people, after all."

"That's easy to understand."

"Do you have someone like that?"

Grant nodded. "I've always been close to my brother. For the longest time we were the only ones that each other had, and we looked out for each other. And we're still very tight."

"It's always good to have someone like that."

"It is," Grant agreed. "Someone who you can go to for advice and to share your problems with."

"Someone who can share your burdens as well?"

"That too. Even if it's just a small amount it helps to have someone take the weight off your shoulders, and we've both done it for each other. I'd do it in a second."

Miranda smiled. "Oh, I envy that, in a way."

"Can't you do that for each other?"

"We both have our own burdens to bear. It seems unkind to force them on someone else."

"That seems... kind of lonely," Grant observed.

"Maybe. But there's a certain beauty to solitude as well."

Grant wasn't sure about that. Evelyn's attitude stuck in his mind. One the surface she might appear fine, but her behavior at some points alarmed him. She kept all her emotions bottled up inside, only releasing them when the pressure became too much. And when she did it, she did it in an almost childish fashion.

And what did that make him? All he had done was to go along with her whims, to indulge her without making any effort to truly understand her problems or try to help her. Her words from that night still stung him. He was both using her and under her heel, following her every order like a puppy.

But yet, with all this disfunction around him he couldn't tear himself away from her. For some call, some reason...

A white knight.

That's what she had called him. A white knight, riding to the rescue of the princess held captive in a tower. Was that it? Was he just living in some kind of fantasy, hoping that he'd heroically save the day for her?

Miranda interrupted his thoughts. "You're an interesting one to talk to. Much better than Evie's previous boyfriends."

"I haven't had a boyfriend," she insisted. "And he certainly doesn't qualify as one."

"Oh I'm crushed," Grant replied sarcastically. "Can't imagine what your exacting standards for a boyfriend might be."

Miranda giggled. "Oh, I'm sorry. Your personal assistants. I forgot that's what you like to call them."

"I'm not the one that came up with the term," she said.

"Who did?" Grant asked, curiously.

"I think it was Josie. Then Rose started to pick up on it, and then it somehow slipped down the line to me. It was a way to have boyfriends that our father didn't approve of."

"But I'm not a boyfriend, so why am I stuck with that title?"

"Because that's the way I want it? And because you actually *are* my personal assistant?" she said. "You seem to have a lot of questions today."

"I think he's good for you," Miranda said with a smile. "I think you two make a good couple. And dad approves of him."

"That's one of the last things I want to hear," Evelyn said.

"Even so..."

"That's enough out of you, thank you very much. And you're one to talk about relationships."

Grant saw the cat jump down to the floor and make its way over to Miranda's seat. She reached down and set it on her lap, then started stroking the back of its head.

"I have no need for one. I'm perfectly content with my life the way it is. But the same isn't true for you, is it? You need companionship."

"Miri, please don't start with this again," she sighed.

"Alright, I'll let it be for now. But I don't think that you're truly going to be happy unless you have some kind of companion to be with you."

"I appreciate the concern, but could you stop trying to play matchmaker with me?"

Miranda smiled. "Oh, I didn't say you have to chose a human companion. Cats are very underrated in that aspect. They're independent, yet they're very loving and affectionate when they want to be."

"Huh, that sounds a lot like someone else," Evelyn commented.

Grant glanced over at her. "Great, steal my joke."

"Consider us even in the snark department."

Miranda laughed. "Really though, you two seem to fit together very well."

Evelyn stood up with a scowl. "That's enough out of you," she said, and left.

Grant stood up as well. "Um, sorry about that?"

"Oh, that's normal. She's not actually all that upset," Miranda told her. "But if I could ask you something?"

"Sure. What is it?"

"Could you look out for her?"

"I'll try."

The smile disappeared from her face.

"No, I mean could you *really* look out for her. Not the window dressing. Not the kind where you're just present around her. I mean, really look out for her well-being."

"Why me?"

"Because you're not a part of this world," Miranda told him. "She's like a princess encased in a crystal, with no way to escape herself. Someone from the outside needs to come along and shatter her prison."

"That sounds... oddly poetic," Grant said.

"Thank you. But there's more to it than just beautiful words. Will you do it?"

"What if she doesn't let me?"

"Then you can't do a thing. But I think she'll open up to you. At least consider it."

Grant nodded. "I will," he said. "Good to visit with you."

"Thank you. Take care until next time."

He gave her a friendly wave and walked away, trying not to scowl. How many more demands was this family going to place on him?

And more importantly, was Miranda's intuition even correct? On the surface Evelyn might be a damsel in distress, but even if that was the case, was he the one to come and save her? Even at his most optimistic Grant could hardly call himself a white knight. His colors were tarnished, his honor in tatters, and he was no better than a dog at this point. Or, as Evelyn had so cuttingly put it, he was just a puppy following her every command.

"Ready to go?" she asked him after he stepped out of the suite.

"I'm ready. Is there anything else for today?"

"Just one thing. There's a charity gala coming up, and I think we both need new outfits for it. So this afternoon might be a good time to go shopping."

"Whatever you wish," he said, following close behind as she walked to the elevators.

Look out for her. Easier said than done at this point. Could he really do that, when he could barely look out for himself?

9

"Ready to go?" Grant asked as he met Evelyn inside her suite.

"I think so. Does this look fine?" she asked.

"It looks good on you," Grant said.

Her dress was fairly simple, made of a bright green fabric with a v-neck top that left her shoulders bare. By itself it hadn't looked like anything special, but it suited her very well, accenting her looks without drawing too much attention to itself.

"Are you just saying that?"

"No, it looks really good on you," Grant said. "I would have told you in the store if it looked terrible."

"Sure you would have," she said with a slight smile.

"I swear, I would have."

"You're lucky that you don't have to do anything complicated. Pick a random suit out of the closet and grab a tie and you're all set."

"I put a little more thought into it than that," he said.

"And with all that you picked charcoal," Evelyn said. "I still think you would have worn a white one."

"Great, stand out and grab everyone's attention, then make a fool of myself when I spill something all over it," he said. "I think that this is safer."

Grant had chosen a dark grey jacket and pants, pairing it with a white shirt. A green tie the same color as Evelyn's dress rounded out the outfit, picked out at her insistence.

"You're no fun."

"I'd like to keep from humiliating myself, thank you very much."

"Oh come on, it would be entertaining. God knows that tonight's going to be insufferable enough."

They headed toward the elevator.

"What exactly is this Gala for? You never gave me much detail on that," Grant said as they stepped inside.

"It's for one of the charitable foundations we run. They're focused on giving scholarships to less fortunate children."

"Does it have a name?"

"Honestly, I can't even remember it."

"It's that important to you, huh?" Grant said dryly.

Evelyn shook her head. "This is going to sound horrible, but it honestly shouldn't even exist. For how much money is poured into the foundation almost none of it goes to the people who need it."

"Who runs it?"

"My father has control but pretty much ignores it. Rose and Josie are the ones in charge, nominally, though they're really just the faces of it. They delegate most of the responsibilities to other people."

"And you?"

"I'm nominally on the board as well, but I'm just there to look pretty and wave at people. Give them a little bit more creditability."

"You sound so cynical about it?"

"Well, I haven't looked at the books at all, but there's millions of dollars going into the foundation every year, yet there's only ten scholarships given out. You can't tell me that you think that's even remotely acceptable."

"Well, there's always overhead."

She snorted. "What kind of overhead costs that much? This barely functions as the bare minimum needed to not lose its nonprofit status."

"Ever thought about doing anything about it?"

"It's crossed my mind, but every time I said something I got the runaround from the other two. So I finally gave up."

"Mm. I understand."

The elevator door opened, and Sam was waiting for them.

"You ride is outside waiting for you," he told them.

They walked outside and climbed in the limousine.

"Any reason why it's just us?" he asked.

"Again, window dressing. If everyone takes a separate

limousine it looks a lot more impressive when we show up. Honestly, I would have rather driven myself, but..."

"But that would just cause more problems," Grant finished. "I really don't envy you at all."

"Yeah, no kidding."

"Even so," he said, "maybe you should start making waves."

"Oh?"

"If you're not happy about the way the foundation is operating, maybe you should take the bull by the horns and try to change things. Or if that's not possible, maybe you can create your own."

"You seem passionate about it."

"Well, I have a reason," he said. "I don't think I would have made it through college without scholarships, so yeah, it's pretty close to my heart."

"Maybe you want to run it then?"

He shook his head. "Maybe I would, but why are you deflecting responsibility? You're clearly not happy about it, so why aren't you doing anything to change things? Are you actually happy where you are?"

She sighed. "Oh, so that's why you didn't immediately follow after me. Miri gave you the 'spread my wings' speech, didn't she?"

"No..."

"Yes...," she said, giving him a look. "You're a terrible liar."

"So what if she did?"

Evelyn shook her head. "I love her dearly, but she's the last person on earth that needs to be talking about that. She can't even do it herself, so why should I listen to her?"

"Just because someone can't see their own weakness doesn't mean they're wrong about seeing it in others," Grant said. "Face it, you're hiding from having to take any responsibility."

"Look who's talking."

"You're just proving my point."

She smiled. "Oh, so you admit it, huh? That you're here because you want to take the easy path, not the one where you're going to have to fight for every inch of ground."

He looked out the window. "So I guess we're in the same boat. Taking the easy path and hiding from having to face our problems. I guess I'm really not the greatest person to pick to try to save you."

"Save me, huh?"

"Her words, not mine."

"Mmm, and she's wrong. She sees only me, and not you. Miri doesn't know you, she doesn't see what's going on under the exterior. So you're supposed to rescue me, huh? Which one of us actually needs saving?"

He didn't have a good answer for her. "So is there anything important for me to do?"

"You're accompanying me tonight. And you're my date for tonight. Keep that in mind."

"Oh, having second thoughts on the boyfriend thing?" he said with a smile, trying to bait her.

"Huh, don't flatter yourself. It'll keep the others away from me."

"So I'm just your shield to deflect all the unwanted attention away from you?" Grant said in a resigned tone. "Oh, that sounds so wonderful. Was that the purpose of your last few assistants?"

"Maybe?"

"Are you sure you're not giving people the impression that you're a lesbian?"

"Nice try, but if that were the case I'd be bisexual, not a lesbian."

"Just asking."

"No, you're just there to keep the insufferable people away," she told him. "Every time I go to something like this without a date someone decides to hit on me, and since I'm trapped there for the duration it's pretty hard to get away from them."

"So once again, I'm your shield."

"Yeah. And don't leave me this time."

"That really wasn't my fault..."

"Well, just make sure it doesn't happen again. Granted, the people here should be a lot more sober..."

"I'll try. But this time don't blame me if it happens."

She grinned at him. "Maybe I will. You have to admit, the aftermath of that was pretty fun."

Grant scowled and looked back out the window. Games. Always more games with her.

Their entry into the gala was met with a considerable amount of fanfare. Grant noticed quite a few members of the press waiting outside, probably from entertainment shows or tabloids.

He fell in beside Evelyn, unsure about how he should act.

"Not going to offer me your arm?" she said quietly.

Grant hastily did so. "Sorry. I wasn't sure-"

"You're my date tonight, remember? Just act normally. You're too stiff."

"Honestly, this is kind of freaking me out, with all the rich people that I don't know."

"Huh, I'm not much better. You're lucky. You're an unknown. I at least have to pretend that I know everyone."

They walked up the carpet and into the gala's main hall, impressive as anything he had seen. The ceiling stretched up for a hundred feet or more, decorated with ornate arches and a plethora of lights. Even the vast crowd seemed tiny by comparison.

"Is Miranda here?" he asked.

"Yes. This is one of the few times she bothers to go anywhere. Apparently this appeals to her sensibilities as well."

"Makes sense. She seems like the educated type."

"She has a masters degree in English from Yale."

"No kidding?"

"Yeah, and it's not honorary."

"Hah," he said with a smile. "I guess that means she's a

rival."

"Oh?"

"I'm a Cornell graduate."

"Oh, I see."

He looked over at her. "Did you go?"

"I did. Not to the Ivy League, though."

That surprised him. "Is there a reason for that?"

"I didn't want to go there," Evelyn shrugged. "To tell you the truth, I went to a state school."

That surprised him even more. "Why? Were you grades not good enough?"

"My grades were fine. I was accepted by Stanford, Harvard, USC, UPenn... you get the idea."

"Where did you end up going?"

"Michigan State."

Grant nodded. "I see."

"So yes, your degree is from a more prestigious school," she said. "Not that it matters. Nepotism has its benefits."

"No kidding. But why choose a state school over all the others?"

"Honestly? Because it pissed my dad off," Evelyn told him. "I had the chance to go somewhere prestigious to make a name for myself, and instead I decided to throw that away to go slum it at a state school."

"I wouldn't exactly call that slumming it..."

"His feelings, not mine. And you know what? I'm glad he felt that way. It was the first time I could defy him and throw it back in his face."

"Did he try to cut you off?"

"Oh he tried, but I had already planned for it and saved tuition money. After my freshman year he figured out he wasn't going to win and gave up."

Grant was about to respond when something caught his eye. A moment later he saw a man walking toward them out of the throng of people.

"Um, speaking over the devil," he said.

"Huh?"

"That's your dad, right?"

Grant heard her swear under her breath. "Yeah, that's him. What's he doing here? He never attends this kind of thing."

"Well, look sharp. Do you want me to do the talking?"

"If you could, that would be great."

He didn't have any more time to think. Grant strode forward to meet the Arno patriarch, trying to put himself between Evelyn and her father. Apparently he was going to be a shield of a very different kind tonight.

"Well, good to see you here son," Robert said, offering his hand.

"It's good to see you as well," Grant said, taking the handshake.

"And Evelyn. Wonderful to see you at this even."

"Yes."

He turned his attention back to Grant. "Now, normally I haven't been able to attend these benefits. Work calls, as I'm sure you'll understand."

"I do," he nodded.

"This year I happened to have the free time, though, so it's good for me to be here. A lot of young, eager faces that will get the opportunity to make something of themselves."

Grant nodded, wondering if there was any subtext behind the words. Was he referring to the scholarship awards, or was he referring to Grant's own predicament?

Robert looked at Evelyn. "I'm sure that you'll have a lot to do to prepare for the awards presentation. I'll leave that up to you."

She nodded. "Thank you. I'll-"

He turned back to Grant. "Well son, let's leave her be while she performs her duties. If you'll walk with me."

Robert turned away and began walking. Grant hesitated and looked back for a moment at Evelyn.

"Go on," she said, though her displeasure was very clear.

Grant followed, feeling a twinge of guilt as he did so. Not even five minutes here and he had already failed his duties for the evening.

They moved through the crowd, occasionally stopping as he greeted various guests and dignitaries. Grant's unease began to grow more and more by the moment. He didn't think for a second that Robert's arrival on the scene was a coincidence, nor was his attempt to separate him from Evelyn. But why would he do that here, of all places?

He followed Robert out of the busy gala hall onto a side porch, currently unoccupied. As Grant looked back over his shoulder he noticed a man in a black suit block the doorway from the inside. Apparently this was to be a private meeting.

"Well son, it looks like you're settling into your current life. How's it treating you?"

"Well enough."

"A good way to put it. Even if you have to sacrifice some of your dignity for the time being."

"I'm sorry?"

"Oh, I know what goes on with those daughters of mine," he said. "If they can find spineless willing fools to go along with their whims then I won't stop them, but I can hardly call them men, can I?"

"I see," Grant replied, trying to give the most neutral answer possible.

"Fools, all of them. But you're a little different, son. You have smarts. You have potential, ambition, drive."

Grant frowned and decided to speak frankly. "I'm still a fool."

"For trusting your business partners too much? Yes son, you're a fool for that. But your mistake didn't kill you, and that means you can learn from it."

"I understand."

"And that's why I need you to stay where you are. The investment arm of our corporation looks like it'll be expanding in the future, son, and I want you to be a part of that."

"Thank you, sir."

"I mean it, son. Those damn fools think they can just

throw away talent just because it has a few bad spots on it. Well, I think different. You've got it, son, and I'm not going to let that go to waste."

"Is that why you came? Just to reassure me?"

"Of course, son. You need to treat people right. And I want to keep you."

"I see."

Part of him was flattered by the amount of recognition he was getting from one of the most powerful men in the financial world, but another part of him felt nothing but unease. The man before him had turned up the charm and was nothing like Evelyn had described him. What was the lie, though, her impression of her father or his seemingly affable nature?

"And then there's the party. Gala. Whatever they call this thing," Robert said. "It's always good to make an occasional appearance at something like this. There's probably a few good ones getting an opportunity here."

"A few," Grant agreed.

A wild idea suddenly popped into his head. He tried to forget about it, thinking at first it was completely insane, but the more he thought about it...

"Um, I noticed something about this when I looked through the details. Especially the finances," he said.

"Oh? Are we not compliant?"

"No, that's fine. But I don't think the foundation is as efficient as it could be," he said.

"That doesn't surprise me," Robert said. "It's not in the

most savvy hands. But continue."

He hesitated. "It occurred to me that the foundation should be able to give out more scholarships. As it is there's only ten issued every year. With the amount of money being brought in it should be able to do three or four times that amount easily."

"And do you have ideas on how to fix that?"

"I have a few," Grant confirmed. "Downsizing the Gala, for one. The amount of money being spent of superfluous things for this could be better spent giving deserving students the scholarships they need."

"Very practical, though the trustees of the foundation are all about fanciness and pomp."

"But that ruins efficiency," Grant argued. "There could be a lot more money spent on the students, and there's advantages to that. It's better public relations."

"Mm, yes."

"And it's going to be more beneficial for the Arno Corporation," he explained. "These students are going into practical majors. Engineering, science, finance, that kind of thing. Doesn't Arno Corp. need young talent like that?"

"Oh yes, that's always a concern for us."

"Then this is a way to profit Arno. In order to maintain their scholarships they had to maintain a certain GPA. But wouldn't that allow you to track them and pick out the most talented? Even if you made them all anonymous and just assigned them numbers you could have that information in your grasp."

Robert chuckled. "Good. Very good, son. You're showing a lot of initiative and smart thinking. Now, what are you going to do about it?"

"Can I make a request?"

"Certainly, son."

"I'd like to be in charge of reforming the foundation up to these standards," he said. "I'll need some help, of course, but..."

"Good, good, showing some of that ambition. I like that. And some good sense. You're not claiming you can do it all yourself. Very well, son. I'll see about putting you in charge of handling the foundation and give you whatever you need. Consider this a bit of on the job evaluation for your real promotion."

"Thank you, sir," Grant said, relieved that his request had gone over well, possibly better than he could have ever hoped. Not only had he been granted permission, but the request itself seemed to put him in even better standing with the Arno patriarch.

Robert clapped him on the shoulder. "Here's your chance to prove your worth, son. Don't disappoint me."

The rest of the gala passed by as a blur. Once the awards ceremony had concluded Evelyn had immediately grabbed him and vacated the premises. Unsurprisingly, she seemed upset on the way back.

Grant tried to smooth over the situation. "I'm sorry. I-"

"It's fine. You couldn't be expected to know that he'd be

there. I just hope you got something out of it."

"Actually, I did," Grant said. He explained their discussion and his request for the rest of the ride.

Evelyn didn't say anything as she listened, and that made him nervous. What did that mean? Approval? Disdain? Acceptance? Something else? Grant wasn't even sure she was actually listening to him.

She didn't say anything as they crossed the lobby, or as they ascended the tower in the elevator. Grant was too afraid to try to break the silence by asking for her thoughts.

"Come on," she said when the doors opened.

"Your room?" he asked.

"Yes."

Grant followed her inside the suite, fairly sure what was going to happen next. As he suspected, Evelyn led him up to the loft.

"Are you going to need me to scrub you down this time as well?" he asked resignedly.

She didn't respond.

"Why are you-"

And suddenly Evelyn had pulled over his jacket and shirt, yanking so quickly that several buttons came off. His tie followed, and then his pants. Before he knew what was happening Grant found himself with his back to the floor, Evelyn on top of him. A second later her dress came off as well.

"Why am I not surprised?" he said.

"So that's it then? He's trying to take you away from

me?"

"That's not-"

"It damn well is," she snapped. "He probably thinks you're the son he never had, and he's trying to take you from me."

"I think you're overreacting," he said.

"Really? So you're falling for him, huh? Listening to his charm and his poisoned words. I don't care if you're using this for your own gain, but you damn well aren't going to sell me put for him."

"It's not like that," Grant protested.

"The hell it isn't! If you're not trying then he is. Well, he can't have you."

She leaned in closer, pinning his arms to the floor with her hands.

"You're mine, you hear me? *Mine.*"

Grant looked up at her in surprise. He though something like this might happen, but he never thought she would be so... forceful.

"What's with you?" he asked. "Are you really that insecure?"

"Hardly."

"I think you are," he insisted. "This happened before. Every time it looks like that someone might try to take me away you turn horribly possessive. Every time you have to dominate me so you feel like you have some sort of control."

"No I'm not."

"Yes you are. You think I'm the one being pulled

between two extremes, but what about you? For someone you're supposedly just casually using you seem to get very jealous about me. Don't pretend that you're just using me and then act like you own me."

"That isn't-"

"It is. It's always about control with you, and it's always about controlling me, because I'm the only one that will let you do it."

Evelyn looked away for a moment. "You're letting me do it right now."

"Well, maybe I shouldn't."

"You won't do anything about it."

Grant pushed his arms free and sat up, then forced her onto her back and pinned her shoulders. Evelyn struggled for a moment, then stopped and looked up at him.

"So what are you planning on doing now?"

What *was* he planning on doing now? Grant had pushed back in the heat of the moment, but after that? He could get up and leave, or…

"You know what? For once you can be the one that submits," he said.

The ghost of a smile crossed her face. "Oh, showing a little bit of backbone now? You really *do* want me don't you?"

"You're one to talk. If you're going to claim me then you need to do more than just saying it."

"I guess that's true." She smiled at him. "You're mine."

Evelyn wrapped her legs around him, sat up slightly

and pressed her mouth to his.

Grant kissed her back, feeling the fiery passion on her lips. Once again he started drowning in the moment, oblivious to everything but her.

10

Grant slowed his pedaling and then came to a complete stop. Sweat dripped down his body. He felt his chest heaving, his legs on fire from sheer exertion. No doubt about it, he had pushed himself far too hard by setting a blistering pace and keeping it up for too long.

His legs felt like jelly as he stepped off the bike, and Grant had to brace himself against the seat for a moment, trying to regain his footing. Once he had managed to steady himself stepped through the door between the training room and the pool.

He didn't have his swimsuit on, but right now all he was wearing was a pair of compression shorts. Grant eased himself into the hot tub one on side of the pool room, sighing with relief as he felt the water wash over him. His legs still burned, but it took the edge off it, at least.

Grant leaned back against the side of the tub, closing

his eyes and trying to relax. Even after all the effort he had just expended on the bike he still felt an immense amount of frustration bottled up inside of him. It had started the night of the charity gala, and the past few days had only made it worst.

Just when he thought he might be figuring Evelyn out she had thrown a curveball at him. Grant hadn't even seen her since that night, and every attempt to contact her had met with little to no success. Every time he messaged her over the past few days asking if she had anything for him to do she had told him he had a free day.

Why? None of it made any sense to him. The one time she had shown anything resembling genuine affection she had immediately withdrawn from him, almost acting like he didn't even exist. Did she regret it? Did she consider it a moment of weakness?"

And if that was true, then why should he even care? If he was just a pawn in her game then why should he feel guilty about using her for his own ends? She had made it clear to him before that she almost expected it to happen.

"You're up early."

Grant's eyes snapped open as he heard the sound of a female voice. For a second he thought it might be her, but as he turned around he spied black hair.

"Good morning," he said to Miranda, noticing she was in a one piece swimsuit.

"Good morning to you. What brings you out so early?" she asked.

"I couldn't sleep and needed to do something," he told her. "What brings you out?"

"Oh, I'm normally up this early. I come here to swim," she said. "If you exercise normally then you must do it later and miss me."

"Yeah, this is pretty early for me."

Miranda set her towel down on a chair beside the pool, then started to fit a swim cap and googles.

"So, no Evie this morning?"

"No."

"Is there something wrong between you two?"

Grant shook his head. "I don't know. I honestly don't. Who can tell with her?"

"Oh dear. That certainly sounds like trouble."

"I know, but I don't even know what's going on. Evelyn won't even see or speak to me at this point."

"Oh? That's a bit unusual."

"No kidding, and I'm not sure what I even did."

He heard Miranda jump into the pool with a surprisingly quiet splash.

"Is it that you don't know what you did, or that you don't want to talk about it? Was it something intimate?"

"You… could say that," he admitted.

He moved to the other side of the hot tub facing the pool, watching Miranda lazily swimming laps on her back.

"Well, I won't pry if you don't want me to. But I'll listen if you want as well. I do know her better than you."

Grant bit his lip, trying to decide whether to share his

thoughts or not. It felt so embarrassing, and yet, if he didn't...

"I'm not sure if I'm reading her right," he said. "She seems to be... very possessive in certain circumstances."

"Oh? Such as?"

"Well, every time I meet your dad, for example."

"I've noticed that he seems to have taken a liking to you," he said. "More than any of Evelyn's others. And definitely more than Josie's or Rose's."

Grant nodded. "I got that impression as well."

"So when you say possessive..."

He sighed, wondering how to word his response. "Let's put it this way, I'm surprised she hasn't put me in bondage gear every time."

"Hm. But it's something similar?"

"Essentially," he replied, trying to dance around the question.

"And was the last time any different?" she asked.

"It was. She tried the same routine, but I resisted a lot more than usual."

"What kind of resistance?"

Grant looked up at the ceiling. "I told her I wasn't going to just continue to submit to her. That if she was going to claim me she needed to do more than just say it."

"Oh. Well, that might have done something. Give me a minute and I might be able to give you some better advice."

Miranda suddenly turned onto her stomach and lunged forward. Grant watched with fascination as she tore through the water at a rapid pace. Clearly she wasn't new to this.

She completed a dozen laps, then slowed down and performed two more before climbing out of the main pool. Miranda took off her goggles and swim cap, then walked over and climbed into the hot tub with him, choosing a seat on the other side.

"So, you many have just put yourself in a bind," Miranda told him.

Grant put his hands up. "What did I *do*?"

"You may have hit a nerve. A very sensitive one."

"I didn't think she had them. She seems to make everything bounce off of her like it's nothing. Except for your dad."

"Oh, there's more sore spots than just him," she explained. "They're just buried very deep."

"And you think I hit one?"

"Yes. Possibly the worst one," Miranda said. "Do you know much about Evelyn's history?"

"She hasn't been very forthcoming about it, and I haven't asked."

"Mmm, then I guess a little bit of explanation is in order. You know that Evelyn's the daughter of my dad's third wife, correct?"

"Yes, that did get mentioned at one point," Grant confirmed. "But I haven't seen her around, so I assumed..."

"That they're no longer together? Yes, that's true in a way, but not what you might think. My mother and Josie's and Rose's mother both divorced him, but she passed away."

"Oh?"

"Yes, and it was fairly unexpected. Evie was only ten at the time."

Grant looked away and sighed. "That hurts. I know how badly that hurts."

"I think that was when everything changed for her," Miranda explained. "She started to become more withdrawn, and it became worse and worse through her teen years. It got better once she went to college, or at least I thought, but..."

"But it didn't actually improve, is what you're saying?"

"I think it manifested itself differently over time. I think she might have been able to hide it, but it's still there."

"I see."

Miranda frowned. "I wish I could have done more, but I was at Yale when it happened and I wasn't home much afterward. I don't know if she was able to connect with Rose and Josie, and I know my father isn't exactly the best person to go to for reassurance and comfort."

"So that's what changed her?" Grant asked.

"I think so. I think as she managed to fight her way back from the edge she became a lot more distant. Like, she put up a barrier between herself and the rest of the world to keep from getting hurt."

A wave of understanding came over him. "And I just tried to smash it down without realizing it. Oh."

"I think that may be why she's distancing herself from

you. She doesn't know how to handle this."

Grant winced. "Is… is there any way to reach her without making it even worse?"

"I think that all depends on her. Nothing you do is going to matter if she won't open herself up to you," Miranda shrugged. She pushed herself up. "But I've stayed for too long. I expect you have other things to do today, so I won't keep you."

"But-"

"If you have more questions I'll be happy to answer them, but I have to feed Midnight first. He's very particular about when he eats."

"So when can we talk again?"

"I have your cell phone number. I'll tell you the time and place to meet," she said, grabbing her towel and walking away.

Grant sat in the hot tub for a few more minutes, silently contemplating his predicament. He understood how badly it hurt to lose someone at a young age, but this? Was this really an excuse for the way she acted? Could he continue to live this way, knowing that he would be distant from her?

The question gnawed at him and wouldn't leave him alone. He exhaled, trying to let out some of the frustration. It did little good. The web around him was getting more and more tangled by the second, and Grant feared he would end up trapped if things kept progressing the way they were currently headed.

Miranda's message arrived later that afternoon.

Meet me in the penthouse.

"Why there?" Grant muttered to himself as he rode the elevator up to the top floor. He would have thought that her suite would have been a better spot.

The doors slid open and he walked toward the penthouse, still apprehensive about the reason for the meeting place. The question still dogged him. Why here? Something about it didn't seem right.

He grabbed one of the double doors, stepped inside...

And was met by the sight of Evelyn as he walked into the main room. Miranda was there as well.

"Oh good, you're here," she said, turning around.

Grant tried to resist the urge to groan aloud. "I thought something was up."

"Oh, you too?" Evelyn said. "Though I didn't think she would resort to this kind of trickery. What's your deal?"

Miranda shook her head. "I'm only doing what needs to be done. You have things that need to be worked out."

"And you're mediating?" Grant asked warily.

She smiled. "Oh no, that's all up to you."

Evelyn scowled. "Why do you-"

Miranda began to walk toward the entrance. "I'm sorry Evie, but this needs to happen."

As she reached the end of the hall she turned around and reached into one of her pockets. It took Grant a moment to realize she had pulled out a chain and padlock.

"You're locked in here for the next three hours. Or something close to it. That should give you plenty of time for you to work out your differences."

Before he knew what was happening Miranda had disappeared out of the doors. It took another second for him to start moving. By the time he pulled on the handles the doors were locked tight.

"That's the last time I ask her for advice," Evelyn said quietly.

Grant turned around and looked at her. "Wait. *You* asked her for advice?"

Evelyn looked back, confusion apparent on her face. "Why, did you?"

"I happened to run into her this morning, and then things came up in conversation..."

She groaned. "Great, so she decided to take matters into her own hands. Wonderful."

Grant walked back into the living room and sat down on a chair. "Um... what exactly did you ask her about?"

"Does it really matter?"

"Apparently it matters enough that we're stuck here together for the next three hours. And about that..."

"What?"

He looked up at her. "Why haven't I seen you in person in four days?"

"I haven't needed you."

"Yeah, I think there's a little more to it than that."

"Fine. I didn't want to see you. Is that good enough for

you?" she asked.

"Why? What did I do?" he demanded

She looked away. "Does it really matter?"

Grant pushed himself up to his feet. "It matters a lot to me, yeah. I don't understand you. I don't understand you at all. One moment you're clinging to me and won't let me go, and the next you don't even want me in your presence. What am I supposed to think?"

"It's just a part-"

"Oh, don't start with that," he snapped. "You know what, I finally think I know what's going on. You built a wall around yourself where you don't have to rely on anyone, where you're not in danger of being abandoned and hurt anymore. And as soon as I started to break through that you pushed back and tried to seal yourself off again."

"Baseless theory."

"Don't give me that. You know damn well that's true, and it goes all the way back to your mother."

Evelyn fixed him with an icy glare. On the surface it appeared calm, but Grant could feel the anger behind her eyes. It was like being stuck in the middle of a blizzard, being pelted by ice and freezing to death.

"Miranda told you that, huh?"

"Maybe."

"And what would you know about it?" she replied.

"I know a lot about it. I had to watch my mom die in front of me," Grant said.

"Then can't you realize how much something like that

hurts?"

He nodded. "Of course I did. Of course it hurt. It hurt more than anything. But that didn't mean I closed myself off from everyone else."

Evelyn looked away. "You don't get it. You're lucky."

"What's that supposed to mean?"

She gazed back at him again. "Even then, you had someone there for you, right? You said that you had your brother. That you had someone you could lean on."

"I did."

"That's why you're lucky. I had no one."

"You at least had someone that shared your grief, right?"

Evelyn walked away and looked out of one of the wide glass windows at the city below. "Did Miranda tell you how it happened? How my mother passed?"

"She didn't."

"Then you're missing a piece. My mother died at age thirty one from sudden cardiac arrest."

"I... see. It must have been surprising."

She shook her head. "It was. At least, for my ten year old self it was. But when I found out what really happened..."

Grant stayed silent, not wanting to say something wrong. Evelyn continued after a moment.

"I didn't realize it at the time because I was so young, but she was suffering from depression for years before her death. She married my father at a fairly young age. Probably out of some romantic notion, but then she lost him to his work. Same as his other two wives. So she fell into depression and looked for whatever fix she could."

"I see."

"And that's it. Later I found out that she had a cocaine addiction, and that's what led to her death."

"Is that why you don't drink?"

Evelyn turned back to him with a steely look. "That's why I don't do any of it. How could I?"

Grant nodded. "I understand. But..."

"But what? So you think I shouldn't be like her? That I should reach out instead of hiding?"

"I think that would be good, yes."

Evelyn shook her head and looked away. "I tried. I really did. I tried. Every time I opened myself up I just ended up getting hurt. The last person I was able to truly open up to was my mom, and..."

"And she was gone?"

"And my father took her away from me," she said. "Oh, he might not have killed her with his own hands, but he caused it. He threw her away like she was nothing. His empire was more important than the woman that loved him."

"But that doesn't mean you'll suffer the same fate," Grant replied gently.

"And who's going to come along and be my knight in shining armor? You?" Evelyn asked, turning around.

Grant bit the bottom of his lip. "It doesn't have to be me. But it's never going to happen if you don't at least try to open up to someone."

"And why should that be you?" she asked. "Why should I believe that you're not going to discard me like all the others? Do you even know what you want?"

"Because I-"

"Spare me the excuses," Evelyn told him coldly. "I know that I'm a stepping stone for you. I know that you have other things waiting for you, and you're concentrating on them. I'm just a means to an end, nothing more. Don't pretend otherwise."

"That's not-"

"Do you think I'm stupid? I know that my father offered you a position, and he's just using this as a way to keep you around until you're ready. Well, fine. That was part of the bargain, wasn't it? That you could use this as a way to rebuild your reputation. So this is just part of the deal."

Grant clenched a fist by his side and didn't respond. He couldn't. An overwhelming wave of shame washed over him. Even if she had agreed to it…

"I haven't made a decision yet," he said defensively. "I'm still not sure whether I'm going to take it or not."

"So you say, but I've seen more than enough people promise me things that never came true. Why should I believe you?"

Why *should* she believe him, Grant thought to himself. What had he shown her to make her believe that he was any different? He wasn't even sure what he actually felt.

"I'm better than you think," he said quietly.

"What?"

He looked her in the eye. "I said that I'm better than you think."

"Again, just words."

"Then give me the chance to put some backbone behind them."

"So you're trying to be my white knight, is that it," she said with a slight smile. "You see the damsel in distress, so you run to save her."

"That's not it."

"That's exactly it, and don't deny it." She looked away again. "I appreciate the concern. Really, I do. But don't feel you have to throw away your dreams and desires just for me. I'll be fine."

For some reason her last line made him angry.

"So that's it?" Grant said. "I shouldn't even try to reach you, because even if I do you won't let me."

"Don't concern yourself with it-"

"The hell I won't!" he interrupted her, the words bursting out of him. "So I'm supposed to go along with your game where you can pretend you're in control? Where you keep your assistants at arm's length and then throw them away before they have a chance to reject you?"

"You're treading over very dangerous ground," she said quietly.

"I don't care. I don't. I'm not going to play this game with you anymore and let you continue to do this. If you're going to keep it up then find someone else."

"So I guess that's it," Evelyn said. "You're finally taking the chance to leave."

"You seem disappointed. I thought you liked it when I showed some backbone."

"Who says I don't like it now?" she asked, though her tone had no conviction behind it.

"You really have a habit of sending mixed signals. First you seem interested, then you pull back and act like it's some joke. Are you really happy that way, or is it just so you don't have to face your fears?"

"Like you know."

"I think I do. It's always about being in control with you. Why can't you let yourself open up for once?" Grant said quietly.

"Why are you so concerned about it?"

"Because it hurts to watch you like this."

"Why?"

"Because… because it does," he said quickly.

Evelyn looked back at him. "Do you love me?"

The question caught him completely off guard. Grant struggled to give an answer, but his lips wouldn't move. His mind raced, trying to come up with something, anything. But…

And then her laugh broke into his thoughts.

"Forget it," she said, looking away with a smile on her face. "Your face was pretty amusing, though."

"Why ask that?" he managed to say.

"Because of the way you're acting. You have everything

you want in front of you. All you need to do is just to play your part, so why is it so hard for you to do that? Is there something else?"

"And you think that's love," he said, looking away.

"Ah, I'm not getting my hopes up," she shrugged. "Makes no difference anyhow. We're going in different directions."

"You sound so resigned to it."

"I'm just a realist. If you can't handle it, there's a way out for you," she said. "If you don't want to be here then I won't hold you back. There's other positions you could be moved to until it's time for you to move up. Take one of those."

"And what about you?"

"I'll manage. It's the same as usual for me."

Grant looked away. "I don't know. I... It doesn't seem right."

"That's a noble view. It's one of your good qualities, truth be told. But it might not be the best thing for you right now."

He looked back at her. "That sounded almost... wistful, in a way."

"Oh, did it?"

Grant paused for a moment, wondering if he should say any more. "You don't want me to go."

"I told you, I'll be-"

"I know what you told me, and I think you're lying," he said forcefully. "You don't want me to leave, but you're afraid that I'll do it anyhow if you ask me to stay, and you don't want to be hurt again."

Evelyn looked at the floor. "It's so easy for you to say. You're not the one left behind trying to pick up all the pieces after everything shatters in front of you."

"So you'll just hide so you can't be hurt again? What kind of life is that?" he demanded.

"It's-"

"It's not fine! How can you say that? You're acting like you have a stone heart, and you know damn well that's not true."

She looked him in the eye. "And what if I let you in? Then what?"

"I don't know. But I do know it's better than what you're living in now."

"You make it sound so easy. Like this is the part of the story where we kiss and all our cares fall away and everything turns out OK, right? That can't happen with me."

"Why?"

Her gaze shifted to an almost pained look. "I've been hurt too many times for it to happen that easily. And what happens then, when you're running into resistance? Are you still going to be the knight in shining armor?"

"I'll try-"

"I've seen you," she continued. "And I think I have a pretty good idea about how you tick. You're driven. You're determined. You'll push for your successes. But the minute those successes are taken away from you then you break. The failure shatters you, and you crumble."

"That's not-"

"That's *exactly* it. Why are you still here? Why didn't you chose something different when you failed at your investment firm? Why did I have to come drag you out of that pit?"

"Because-"

"Because you can't handle failure. You can't handle the fact that your success suddenly evaporated in front of you, and you have to keep chasing it, trying to get it back so you can feel your worth again."

"That's not true," he protested.

"Oh, then why are you still here, prostituting yourself so you can get back in their good graces and take your prestige and success back, huh?"

Grant looked down at the floor. "Even if that's true, why couldn't I have changed my mind? Didn't you say that was happening?"

"And what will keep you from changing it back?" Evelyn asked. "I'm not foolish enough to think that opening up to you is going to be easy. Not after all the times I've been hurt before."

"I know. But-"

"It's too easy for you," she interrupted him. "You think you just need to snap your fingers and it'll magically happen."

"I don't. I know it's going to take a lot more than that."

"And what happens if you think that your can't

succeed? What happens when I open myself to you, only for you to abandon me because you can't handle the prospect of failure? What then?"

Grant looked at her. "That's a low blow."

"I don't care. It needed to be said."

"What am I supposed to do? You're clearly not OK with the way things are. How am I supposed to leave you like this? How low do you think I am?"

"I don't doubt you have good intentions," Evelyn said. "But what happens when you realize you can't be a white knight? What stops you from taking the other path?"

"I'm better than you think I am."

"Once again, we're back to words. And there's not much behind them."

"Then let me prove it," Grant replied, the frustration continue to grow. Why did he even care at this point? Why, despite all the opposition, was he still trying to push forward?

"You're never going to stop this, are you?"

"Probably not."

She sighed. "I'll think about it. I know that's not the answer you want, but it's the best one I can give you at the moment."

"OK."

"And I'm not going to hold you back. If you think it's best to leave now, well, I won't stop you. It's not fair to drag you down with me."

"I'm not leaving now," Grant insisted. "Not when I can

see what's happening in front of me. And I'm not going to abandon you."

"Don't throw away your hopes and dreams out of a misguided sense of nobility. I'll be fine."

Grant clenched a fist by his side. "You say that, but..."

"I mean it."

He looked her in the eye. "I know you do. And honestly, it hurts a lot to know you feel like that."

"It's perfectly normal."

"No it's not. You go through life expecting everyone to hurt or leave you? How is that even remotely normal?"

"I've managed so far."

"The hell you have." He took a deep breath. "I'm no saint, but I've managed to overcome a lot of horrible things in my life. But I had to open up to other people and let them help me."

"And that just happened for you, huh?"

Grant shook his head. "No. I was a pretty angry and bitter teen. I spent years going to a psychologist, and I still might not be fully healed. I *know* I'm not. But I'm in a far better place than I would be if I just kept it all in."

"So you're saying that I need to be put in a shrink?"

"That's not even close to what I'm saying, and you know it," he scowled. "But did you ever actually see someone about it?"

Evelyn didn't give him a response.

"I'm assuming that's a no?"

"Why does this even matter to you?" she asked.

"Because I can't just sit by and watch this happen."

"Still trying to play the white knight, huh?"

Grant shook his head again. "You know what? I really don't care if that's supposed to be an insult. I can't just sit here and let this happen when I can do something about it."

"So you're just going to abandon your original plan out of the blue, is that it? Do you really even believe that?"

He looked away. "I do."

"Well, I believe you think that way right now. Whether that changes is an entirely different story. But I at least appreciate it. Just don't get your hopes up."

Grant looked at her. "And that's what you're doing. Trying not to get your hopes up."

She shrugged. "Well, from my point of view that's the prudent course of action. But that could always change. And besides, it isn't so bad now, is it?"

"Well…"

"Excluding the past few days. I promise I won't ignore you like that again. Not unless you deserve it."

"I appreciate that." He looked up at the clock in the corner of the living room. "We're stuck in here for over two hours. How long did she think this was going to take?"

"Who knows what she was thinking." Evelyn sat down on one of the couches. "Well, we're here already. I have to admit, the past few days were pretty boring without you."

"Does that mean what I think it means?"

"What do you think it means?" she asked with a smile.

"Do you seriously want to screw right now? Right after

that argument?"

"Well, there's nothing else to do for two hours." She grinned at him. "Besides, like I told you, you're better in bed when you're angry."

"I can't believe that you're convincing me to do this," he said as she reached up for him.

That was the end of his resistance, though.

11

Grant sat in front of his computer, looking over financial statements for the foundation. It had been a while since he had dealt with something this intricate, so at first it took him a while to get through the first set of pages. Steadily, though, he picked up speed and began to sift through the information.

"So how does it look?" Evelyn asked as she sat down beside him on the couch. She set a large bag on the coffee table in front of them.

"What the heck is that?"

"I figured it was getting late, so dinner would be good."

He looked closer at the bag.

"Chinese takeout?"

"What, you have a problem with that?"

Grant shook his head. "No, I'm perfectly fine with it. It's just, well, it really doesn't fit with what you normally seem like."

"And what's that supposed to mean?"

"You know what, I think I'm going to just stop talking right now before I dig myself a bigger hole."

"Good choice."

Grant nodded and continued looking at the screen. At least they seemed to be back to normal, or at least what passed for normal between them. He didn't think they were any closer to a resolution, but at least the tension between them had decreased substantially.

And that also gave him the opportunity to properly concentrate on his project. Even if it was little more than a hobby at this point he could use it to sharpen his skills, and maybe help a few people in the process.

"So, what's going on with this?" she asked again.

Grant leaned back into the couch and stretched. "Well, it's about what you'd expect. There's a lot of money going into the foundation, and a lot of it going out. Problem is, I don't think that it's going to the places it's needed."

Evelyn pulled a box out of the bag and opened it up, then grabbed a pair of chopsticks. "Mmm. So what's the cause of it?"

"Well, the amount of money spent on the gala certainly doesn't help. According to the records they spent over two million dollars for this year's ceremony alone."

"Not a surprise," she said, slurping up a mouthful of noodles. She paused for a moment and chewed. "It's never simple with those two. They always need to have the biggest, prettiest things around, no ifs, ands or buts."

"I get why they want to do that. It attracts a lot of attention, which brings in more donations," Grant said. "Problem is, there's a lot of ways to do that, and they're probably a lot cheaper as well."

"Plus the scholarship itself should be prestige enough. Who cares how many bells and whistles go along with it?"

"Huh, that's surprising austere from you."

Evelyn poked him with her chopsticks. "What's so surprising about it? Look at me. I'm sitting here in sweatpants and an eight year old t-shirt downing takeout, not in a ballgown daintily eating caviar."

"OK, OK, forget I said anything."

"Anything else interesting?"

"Well, there's quite a bit of staff overhead. Probably more than there should be, considering the amount of scholarships that actually go out."

"Again, not shocked. Neither of them went to school for business."

"What'd they go for?"

Evelyn made a face. "Fashion design, or something like that. Not to knock it, but that's not exactly something to prepare them for running a huge charitable foundation."

"But you said that they delegate responsibility?"

"Yeah, it's mostly to their personal assistants. Why?"

"You'd think that they'd want to make it more efficient," he shrugged. "Or at least, I think they'd have enough incentive to make themselves look good."

"Like I said, this kind of thing is window dressing. It's a way to make it look like they're doing something good without actually doing anything."

Grant frowned. "And the people who could use the help don't get it because they have to play around."

"Hey, I don't like it either."

He scrolled through the list. "And that's about it. There's a lot of money going in and out of the foundation, but too much of it is going to places where it shouldn't. I think the gala is the worst culprit."

"Do you have a financial breakdown for that?"

Grant nodded and opened up another file. "Yeah, it's here. Again, there's a lot of various expenses, but a lot of them probably aren't necessary."

"Let me see that," she said, setting her box and utensils down on the coffee table.

Grant handed over his laptop and reached into the bag and pulled out another box. The contents smelled good, with a spicy edge, but he didn't recognize the dish.

"No idea what this is," he said.

Evelyn reached over and pulled out a chunk with her chopsticks. "It's mapo doufu. Try it. It's good."

Grant fished out a plastic fork from the bag and sampled a bite. He enjoyed the taste, though the heat made him wince for a moment.

"Ah, that's pretty spicy," he said, reaching for a bottle of water sitting on the coffee table.

"That makes sense. I ordered the hottest one."

"Why?"

"Because it's the only way to get real mapo doufu? Everywhere else tones the heat down too much."

"Anything else that won't torch my tastebuds?"

"Huh, probably. Dig around some more."

Grant reached inside of the bag again and pulled out another box, noticing that there were several more boxes inside. "How much food did you order?"

"Enough to get good samples."

"Seriously, do you need that much?"

"I'm not going to eat it all at once. I do have a kitchen in my suite, and leftover Chinese food is a good late night snack."

"OK, point taken." He opened the next box and pulled out a piece of meat."

"Mm, good choice grabbing the char siu box," Evelyn said, again reaching over and taking a piece with her chopsticks.

"Are you actually looking at anything, or are you just eating?" he asked.

"You say that like I'm incapable of multitasking," she replied.

The char siu was far less spicy than the mapo doufu with a sweet and salty flavor. Grant hadn't eaten since noon, and he dug in.

"So, this is interesting," Evelyn said. "It looks like quite a bit of money was paid out to a company called Visions Consulting."

"Why a consulting firm?"

"Hold on a second, let me look." She clicked open another file and scanned it. "So apparently it's a headhunter or middleman company of some sort. It says they were hired to make arrangements for the gala. Securing the location, arranging catering, the band, decorations, that kind of thing."

"Well, depending on the cost that might be for the best. It streamlines the process, at least."

"Maybe that's true. But I'm not sure it's so innocent."

Grant frowned. "What makes you say that?"

"Because the foundation has been around for a decade. I don't remember them making any changes, either. When I was trying to push for an overhaul a few years ago I remember looking at the financial statements. I think they pretty much use the same people every year. I'd have to look again, but I think that's the case."

"OK, so what?"

"I don't remember seeing anything about this consulting firm. Again, I could be wrong about it, but a look at some of the other financial statements could shed some more light on it."

"So what are you thinking?"

"Fraud, most likely."

"Why jump to that conclusion?"

"Because it's the only thing that makes sense," Evelyn said. "If they use the same people every year, why bother giving all this money to the consulting firm when they could just use a single staff member or an intern to do the work?"

"Could it just be laziness?"

She snorted. "I don't think Rose and Josie are *that* lazy. This is incredibly dumb."

"So you suspect foul play?"

"I think that's the only good explanation," she said. "The consulting firm doesn't make sense unless it's being used as a shell company of sorts."

Grant frowned, a familiar feeling grabbing hold of him. "So you think it's money laundering?"

"More or less. The consulting firm could be completely legitimate, so to speak. It could be completely legal, but then the question is who's operating it?"

"So you think someone on the inside of the foundation is contracting out to the firm, which they have a stake in, and then pocketing the cash from that?"

"I think that's very likely. Of course I have no way to prove, that, but that's what I think is going on." She handed the laptop back over to him and picked up one of the boxes.

Grant took it from her, a feeling of frustration coming over him. It was happening again. Fraud occurring right behind his back, and it took someone else to remove the blinders and point out the cold, ugly facts to him. Evelyn's father might say that he had talent, but had he really learned anything from his previous failure? He hadn't even spotted the discrepancy, while it took Evelyn only a quick glance to pick it out.

That thought disturbed him more than anything else.

"So," she asked, "what do you want to do about it?"

"I guess it needs to be reported?" Grant shrugged.

"And who's going to do anything about it? If my suspicions are correct then it's probably legal, at least on the surface. Might be fraud, but if they were smart they took pains to cover their tracks."

"So you're just going to let it go?"

"Of course not," Evelyn said. "Something's going on here, and I want to find out what."

"And once you do?"

"If they're cheating us then they're going to get the appropriate punishment. It's not good for people to think that they can just steal from us."

"Us?"

"I'm on the trustee board. That gives me a bit of responsibility for this, at least. None of the others are going to do anything about it."

"Do you think they could be involved?"

"*Tch*. Rose and Josie aren't capable of doing something this complex. They're too busy collecting a million pairs of shoes and snorting everything in sight."

"But your explanation makes it pretty simple, or at least not overly complicated."

"So? How does that conflict with my point in any way."

Grant sighed. "You really aren't nice to your sisters, you know that?"

"Damn right, and don't care."

"Seems to be your motto."

"Maybe I'll put that on a t-shirt," she replied.

He smiled. "OK, I could totally see you wearing that."

"Anyhow, I think we're going to need to take a closer look at this entire thing. If at all possible we'll need to get the financial records for the foundation, possibly dating back to the inception."

"We?"

"Do you have a problem with that?"

He shrugged. "Honestly no, but you didn't seem like you were interested when I told you about it."

"Look, I was in a really bad mood that night. And can't a girl change her mind?"

"The healthy answer for me is yes, right?"

She smiled at him. "There you go. You're trained so well. Puppy."

Grant ignored the jibe. "So you're on board for this, huh?"

"Yeah, why not? It's interesting, at least, and it's not like I have anything else to do. Besides, you could probably use another set of eyes for this."

The comment was innocent enough, but it rankled him nonetheless. Once again his shortcomings were being made very clear. Could he really be called a talent at this point when he was stuck relying on someone else?

But he tried to push those frustrations aside. They weren't Evelyn's fault, and Grant wasn't going to turn down help from someone who knew what she was doing. And it might help her a bit, to have a concrete goal to work toward.

"Glad to have your help," he said.

"Right. So we're going to need to get records, and you might want to convey some of your suspicions to my father as well."

"Why don't you do it?"

"Because he's not going to listen to me, because I was born with the wrong parts?"

"How did he get so rich if he wasn't willing to employ or listen to women?"

"The lower levels of management don't have those kinds of problems. And he had already built a pretty big empire by the time that women really started making their push in the business world."

Grant frowned. "Wait, how old is he?"

"Right now? He's seventy five."

"He's that old?"

"Yeah. How do you not know that? Did you not pay attention to anything outside your own bubble of the business world?"

"No, it's just... I was under the impression that he was the son of the founder of the Arno Corporation. He doesn't look that old."

"Nope, one and only founder."

"I see. That's... enlightening."

"Good to know." Evelyn grinned at him. "I'm the product of that seventy five year old man."

"Um, OK?"

"Just something to think about. You know, when we're

having sex, or something like that."

Grant winced. "Thank you very much for that image. I see you have no problem mentioning your father when it comes to trolling me. Did you have fun making that up?"

"I didn't make it up. One of my former personal assistants did."

"Oh."

"Yeah, he didn't last very long after that. No big loss, though. Very pretty to look at, but sometimes I wasn't sure whether he had brain matter or rocks up there."

"I'm glad I rank so highly. Though I'd have thought you would have preferred men like that, since they're a lot easier to control."

"No fun in that. No excitement."

"Is that what you're calling those arguments we've had?" Grant replied dryly.

"Let's not start on that tonight. There's a lot more for us to think about. Like you reporting everything to him, right?"

"Right. What should I tell him?"

"Don't go into too much detail, but I'd at least say that you're concerned about some kind of discrepancy. He's probably going to be curious if you ask for more records, so you at least need a reason for it."

"Understood."

"And you can even take credit for this. It gives you another feather in your cap."

"Doesn't that bother you?" he asked.

"Doesn't what bother me?"

"That you're giving me all the credit for things you've spotted. Isn't that a little bit unfair?"

Evelyn shrugged. "Really, who cares?"

"I-"

"Not everyone feels the need for success like you do," Evelyn said. "If this happens, who cares about the credit?"

"It's just… I don't know, it just doesn't feel right to me. You should be able to show off your abilities."

She smiled at him. "Look, I appreciate the concern, but it's fine. I've given up any hope of doing anything to impress my father, and I'm better off for it. He's never going to accept me anyhow, so why should I even bother?"

"That seems… defeatist."

"I'd call it pragmatic," Evelyn shrugged. "Anyhow, that's what you need to do. Get your hands on the documents we need so we can look over them. And after that we can figure out what's going on."

Grant couldn't help smiling.

She gave him a quizzical look. "What?"

"Nothing."

"Obviously it's something? Now, what is it?"

"It's just, well..."

"Come on, spit it out."

"Well, I guess this is the most relaxed that I've every seen you. You're not trying to project an image or put up a front. You're just being yourself."

Evelyn looked away. "Is it really that big of a deal?"

"It's just something I noticed. And I think it's good. It

suits you well."

"Oh?"

"Yeah. You're cute when you let your guard down."

Evelyn went silent for a moment. "Well, it's better than making jokes about my father's age," she replied.

Grant thought he saw her blush, but maybe it was just a trick of the light.

12

"So you want all of the financial records from the foundation, son. May I ask why?"

Grant hesitated for a moment, trying to figure out the best way to word his request. He had gone over it a dozen times in his head, but now, speaking over the phone his mind had gone blank for a moment. How should he do it without causing too much of a fuss?

"Everything seemed normal at first glance, but there was something that caught my attention," he said carefully. "I'm not sure if there's anything going on, or it's just my imagination, but I thought I should take a look, just in case."

"Good. Very good. Seems like you're learning, son," Robert said on the other end of the line. "Very well. I'll have them sent to you so you can take your look. If you see anything suspicious then I'd appreciate if you'd let me know."

"I will, sir. Thank you."

Grant breathed a sigh of relief when he hung up. He hadn't expected to run into much trouble, truth be told, but every conversation with the head of he Arno Corporation was intimidating, no matter how affable he might seem.

But Grant definitely had his attention. Normally something like this would be handled by a lower level employee or officer. Such things were beneath someone of his stature. Yet here he was, requesting that Grant report directly to him and keeping close tabs on his progress.

Robert had said something about this being an on the job evaluation, but Grant hadn't thought much about those words until now. Now he knew they weren't just for show. He had some notoriety, and that could be the opening he needed.

But could he really be happy about that? Grant hadn't been the one to spot the discrepancy. Evelyn might not care about getting credit, but the fact remained that it was her, not him that had started the ball rolling in this case. For all he had been through, for all his lack of oversight and overabundance of trust had hurt him, he really had learned nothing from the experience.

And what would that mean in the future? Even if this did turn out well, even if he was able to get into the position he wanted and needed to salvage his career, would it be worth it? He'd still be the same person, unable to spot the machinations happening right under his nose.

Grant wasn't exactly naive about what that meant for him, either. The blind spot had hurt him once, and he had little doubt that it would catch up to him sometime in the future. Could he really stay on his current course, ignoring the potential disaster in front of him? It might be best for him to stay where he was for now.

What happens if you think you can't succeed?

Evelyn's words from their argument in the penthouse still haunted him. He hated to admit it, but they cut far, far deeper than he thought they would have. They seemed to be proving themselves prophetic, though. Grant had serious misgivings about his ability to perform in the position being offered to him, even if he had full confidence from the Arno patriarch.

And was that it? How could he go forward into something where he knew he couldn't win?

Every time you meet failure you crumble.

Her words kept haunting him.

You can't handle the fact that your success suddenly evaporated in front of you, and you have to keep chasing it, trying to get it back so you can feel your worth again.

Grant felt the frustration rising inside of him. What did she know about it? She had been born into a wealthy family, put into this position by birth. His life had been stacked against him from the beginning. He had fought for everything he had become, even in the face of overwhelming odds. He had overcome, and he had built something out of it all.

But then…

The betrayal had hit him hard. Grant had thought he

was immune to that kind of hurt after going through so much turmoil in his childhood, but his partners' treachery had completely flattened him. For the first year he had been a mere shell of a man.

Why are you still here? Why didn't you chose something different when you failed at your investment firm? Why did I have to come drag you out of that pit?

Grant gritted his teeth, trying to keep his emotions in check. He wanted to deny it, but…

But was she right?

Could he really keep chasing after his career, with all evidence to the contrary piling up? Could he really keep heading the way hc was going?

But the other option…

Even after her piercing deconstruction of his motivations, Evelyn had still pushed him away. She pushed him toward the path that he seemed to desperately need to travel, even if he knew what lay ahead.

He could turn away from it, but…

I'm not foolish enough to think that opening up to you is going to be easy. Not after all the times I've been hurt before.

He wanted to do it. He wanted to try to break down the wall that Evelyn had built between herself and the world. She might claim to be fine, but Grant wasn't buying her excuse. He could here it, could see it, could feel it every time he was with her. She was trapped, and she wanted a way out.

He wanted to break the wall down so badly. More than anything Grant hated to see someone trapped. He remembered being trapped in his own prison, living in constant fear. When the walls had finally broken down the elation he had felt was like no other.

What happens when I open myself to you, only for you to abandon me because you can't handle the prospect of failure? What then?

"Why can't you take a chance?" Grant muttered to himself.

Could he really do it? Could he really try, knowing that he was going essentially going up against a stone wall, trying to beat it down with his fists and nothing else? Was it worth it if she kept shutting herself off from him, pulling back every time he tried to reach her?

Do you love me?

Grant flopped down on his bed and put his face into a pillow. He let out a long, muffled yell of frustration.

He didn't know. He didn't know the answer to that. A romantic would say yes, he did love her, but Grant felt far too cynical about their relationship now to believe that. Could he really be in love with a woman that he barely even knew, one that tried to keep her true self a mystery to him? Could he really say that he loved her, or was he just infatuated with the idea of her?

So you're trying to be my white knight. You see the damsel in distress, so you run to save her.

Grant sighed again. The way she had said that had been so... so casual, so cynical. The thought of it made him angrier than it should have, but he wasn't sure who he felt angrier at, her for saying it, or himself for even making her think that way.

Was this all just some fantasy for him? That he could ride in on the proverbial white horse and sweep her off her feet? That he could somehow overcome years upon years of her isolation, her pain, her loneliness in such a short time?

It's too easy for you. You think you just need to snap your fingers and it'll magically happen.

He wanted to deny it, but…

But what happens when you realize you can't be a white knight? What stops you from taking the other path?

He didn't have an answer. He could protest, plead, promise, but he couldn't give her anything concrete. And why should she even believe him? A short while ago he had been resisting her, struggling for dominance while biding his time. Could she really believe that he had changed that quickly? Could *he* believe it?

Grant heard his phone go off beside him and reached over, hoping that he wouldn't have to see her today. That hope was immediately dashed.

Come to my room.

"Perfect timing," he muttered, trying to resist the urge to throw his phone in frustration.

Delaying wasn't going to make it any better, though. Grant pushed himself up and headed for her suite as ordered.

"What did you want from me?" he asked when she met

him in the entryway. He noticed she had her purse with her.

"I'm bored, so I'm going out. And since you're my personal assistant, you're coming with me."

"Need a bag carrier, huh?"

"We're probably not going to do a lot of shopping, so no. I just want someone with me."

"And I'm it?"

She gave him a puzzled look. "Why? Who else do you think would be doing it?"

Grant shook his head. "Never mind."

"What?"

"Nothing. It's nothing."

"You're not still upset about our conversation in the penthouse, are you?"

"That's all that was to you? A *conversation*?"

"That's what we did, right?"

Grant took a deep breath, trying not to lose control. "I don't get you."

"You say that a lot."

"Well, I think that a lot. Do you really think that, or are you just trying to play it cool?"

Evelyn looked away. "Now's not the time for this."

"Fine, we can deal with it later. But I'm not just going to be able to ignore this."

She shrugged. "OK, fine. But I'm still bored, so we're going somewhere."

"Whatever," he shrugged as he fell in beside her on the way to the elevator.

Evelyn suddenly spoke up once they were inside. "But it's not like I'm not listening to you."

Grant looked over at her. "I didn't say anything."

"You were thinking it."

"I really wasn't..."

"Nice try."

"No, I wasn't. But clearly you were."

For a moment Evelyn struggled to say something. Grant looked away, a smile on his face.

"And now you're flustered about it. That's all the proof I need."

"Think what you want."

"Oh, I will."

Their car was waiting for them out front. Both of them sat in silence as they rode toward their destination. Grant wondered where they were going if they weren't going to do much shopping. What else was there to do? Evelyn hadn't shown a lot of interest in many things outside of the tower.

When they finally stopped Grant looked out the window in confusion. A huge building lay before him, but this one sprawled out for a great distance, several acres at the very least. And as he saw the sign, there was no mistaking it.

"Wait, the aquarium? Why here?"

"Why not?" she shrugged. "It's something to do."

"It's... I don't know, it just seems out of the ordinary. Like, well..."

"Like it doesn't fit with what you think of me? Is that what you're saying?"

"You know what, I'm just going to stop talking right now."

A slight smile crossed her face. "Another good choice."

They stepped out at the entrance and headed inside. Grant looked around a bit as they waited at the ticket counter. Even for a weekday the place was busy: families, students, an occasional couple.

"Ever been here before?" she asked.

"This is the first time. It's somewhere I've wanted to go, but I never really got the chance."

"Well then, now you're here. Come on."

"Where are we headed first?"

"Well, the polar exhibit is first, so that's probably the best place to start."

"Right behind you," Grant said. Some of the tension between them still remained in the air, but the change in atmosphere had lessened it quite a bit. He decided that he was going to try to forget about everything and just enjoy himself while he could.

Evelyn stopped in front of a large glass window in the first tunnel, pausing to watch the penguins diving in and out of the water, swimming, resting, preening.

"Not a care in the world," she said.

"Sorry?"

"They don't have a care in the world. They're taken care of here. They don't have to face the dangers they would in the wild. All they need to do is stay in their cage and they're safe."

Grant frowned. "Sounds like you're trying to make an awkward metaphor there."

Evelyn shrugged. "Maybe, maybe not. Maybe I'm just rambling on about nothing."

"But that's how you feel?"

She kept looking at the penguins. "I don't know."

"Is that such a bad thing?"

"Some people say that being locked up in a cage is bad for you. Or them."

"And is one of them standing next to you right now?"

"Oh, I don't know."

She began walking further down the tunnel. Grant followed behind, wondering if she had brought him here because of an ulterior motive. Was she just here to entertain herself, or was there a greater point to it?

"I don't think this is a bad thing," Grant said. "I don't think that it's a good thing either."

"So you think the answer is somewhere in the middle? The golden mean?"

The tunnel descended further, toward a chamber with windows on three sides. As they stepped into it Grant could see seals dancing through the water, swimming freely.

"I don't think that's quite right," he said. "I don't think it's necessarily wrong for them to be here, where they're safe. But I don't think it's right to keep them all in cages either."

"Now who's the one trying to make the really awkward metaphor?" she said with a smile.

"Look, I didn't major in English like Miri, OK?"

"Ah, you're trying, at least."

"So what about it?"

He looked at her again. "What about it? I'm not quite sure what you're getting at."

Evelyn let out a sigh. "You seem so determined to break down the wall around me, as you say, but is that really the best thing?"

"And that's the metaphor you're trying to make?"

"Mm, I guess."

Grant gazed back into the exhibit, watching a seal flip around as it swam by. "I'd tell you that people aren't just animals, and that your metaphor is imperfect."

"I guess."

"And that's about it," he shrugged. "I don't know about you, but we seem to be going in reverse here."

"I'm not sure what you mean..."

"Isn't this something we'd normally do on a first date? You know, instead of what we actually did."

A smile played about her face. "Oh, who says that this is a date?"

"Come on, that's what it looks like."

Evelyn continued walking. "I guess I don't really know. I haven't connected well with other guys before. You're probably more experienced than me."

Grant frowned. "I don't know about that," he said. "My love life hasn't actually been all that successful, as you can probably tell."

"I'm surprised that you're still single," she said.

"It's just something that never happened," he explained. "I had to dedicate most of my time to the firm. I dated, I had a few girlfriends, but they were nothing more than casual flings at most. Any time any of them wanted something more I wasn't able to give them the attention they needed."

"Career over relationships, huh?"

He bit his lower lip for a moment. "Yeah, I guess. I know that probably doesn't sit well with you."

"Why? You didn't make them promises you were never going to keep, right? You were at least up front with your priorities," she said.

"I guess."

"But that's a little different from where you are now," Evelyn said. "Right now I'm not really clear about your intentions."

"I thought I was pretty clear about them."

"Maybe in your mind, but I'm not even sure that you know."

Grant wondered if she had picked up on the struggle going on inside of him. As far as he could tell he hadn't done anything to tip her off, but if nothing else she was fairly perceptive. Even if he tried to hide it Grant wasn't sure how long he could actually conceal his thoughts.

"I'll admit one thing to you," Evelyn said. "I'm not sure what to do."

That admission surprised him. "Oh?"

"Yes. Your plea was rather convincing, actually. I thought I was immune to them, but..."

"But you do feel something?"

She stopped in front of another exhibit and looked through the glass at the polar bear inside. "Maybe. Maybe not. Maybe I'm just confused about the whole thing."

"Always maybes with you."

"I'm not sure what I feel," she said frankly.

Grant didn't respond. He couldn't exactly argue. He felt the same way about her. Should he keep pushing forward, focusing on regaining his old life, or should he stop and try to make a new one with her, knowing that the chances of success were very, very slim?

"But if you're not sure what you feel..."

"I'm not sure what I feel, and that's that. It's not going to change anytime soon. I told you that already."

"I understand that."

"So are you really going to wait around, hoping for something that may never happen?"

Grant looked away. "I'm not sure how I feel either."

"Then we're at an impasse."

"Seems like it."

They reached the end of the exhibit and headed out into the main concourse. Grant was about to ask where she wanted to go next when Evelyn grabbed his hand. His heart skipped a beat for a moment.

"Come on," she said, leading him forward.

Grant followed, wondering where she was going and what she had in store for him. She wove her way around the crowd in the concourse, heading for another exhibit on the other side. Before he knew what was happening they were inside the next passage.

And suddenly, he felt very, very small.

Evelyn had just led him into another tunnel, only this was made out of solid glass. A vast expanse of water stretched out above them and to both sides. Soft light danced over them, tinted blue.

And Grant watched with wonder as a giant passed over them, a huge beast with a white belly. It swam regally though its tank, master of its own domain. Another shape followed close behind it.

"Whale shark tank," Evelyn explained as they walked further down the tunnel.

It extended for a long distance, probably about thirty or forty yards, then branched off at a ninety degree angle and ascended further up the wall of the tank. As they stepped further up Grant was able to get a good glimpse of both leviathans from above.

"That was it," she said. "Out of everything here, that was the one thing that always amazed me the most. Looking up into the ocean at one of those and realized just how tiny and insignificant I was."

Something compelled him forward, and Grant put an arm around her. To his surprise she made no move to stop him.

"We may be tiny," he said, "but that doesn't mean that we're alone."

Grant felt her squeeze his hand. "You should probably

stop saying that," she said. "I might start believing you."

"So Evelyn took you to the aquarium yesterday?" Miranda asked the next morning.

"She did," Grant nodded, relaxing in the hot tub after another round of cycling.

"Good. She needs to get out more."

"You're one to talk."

Miranda giggled. "But I'm a home body. She's not. And the aquarium. That's very interesting."

"Why's that?"

"Because she hasn't been there for years. It was one of her favorite places in the world, but she stopped going."

"When?"

"When she turned ten."

It didn't take him long to make the connection.

"So wait, she took me to a place that she hasn't been in years, probably because it makes a painful connection to her mom?"

"Yes, that's about right."

That made him think. Despite what she might be saying, despite all the warnings she had given him, she was at least trying to open up to him a bit.

And that gave him hope.

13

"Take a look at this," Grant said, handing a stack of papers to Evelyn.

She flipped through them, skimming through the charts and notes. "So I'm right?"

"Yeah, you're right. Something's up with the consulting firm," he told her. "Although that means there are a lot of other questions that need to be answered."

"The main one being who's the one causing all these problems?"

"That's the biggest one. Trouble is, I don't really know how to go about it. We need to get to the bottom of this, but I want to be circumspect about it. There's no use trying if we tip them off."

"In a way there is," Evelyn said.

"How so?"

"Well, if they get word of what we're doing they'll

either stop, or more likely, they'll make a run for it so they don't end up in prison," she explained. "So that takes care of the problem."

"But it really doesn't."

"Sure, if you're obsessed with punishing them."

Grant looked over at her. "Don't you think that they should pay for costing people so much money?"

"Well yeah, I'm not glad they did it, but pragmatically speaking it might be best just to get rid of them, if that's the only good option that presents itself. We can't suddenly reverse the fact that there were only ten scholarships in previous years."

"I'd like to do both, if possible."

"Mmm, we'll see if it is. I would be wary about it, though. Spending too much time trying to balance both might mean you succeed with neither."

He saw her point, but Grant believed that justice needed to be served.

"So this started happening three years ago, and it's involved hundreds of thousands of dollars," he said. "So that probably means that someone came in during that time."

"Or it means that they were already in place and decided to start embezzling money," she said.

Grant ran a hand through his hair. "OK. Now the question is how we get to the bottom of this and narrow things down."

"Hire an auditor."

"That was my thought too, but we'd have to pay for it

out of pocket. Your father wasn't keen on letting us do it."

"Huh, that's unusual. He's usually all over corruption."

"Yeah, well, I think he's using this as a way to test me."

Evelyn snorted. "Of course. There's always ulterior motives when he's involved. And I'm pretty sure he really doesn't care about the foundation, so if you miss things then there's no big loss."

"You don't have to be involved," Grant said. "This is my job, or at least, it was something he gave to me. And you don't need to-"

She interrupted him. "Once again, I don't care if you take the credit or not. I'm here because I'm interested. I see what's going on and now I'm curious why it's happening. So I'm staying."

"Fine, but you might have to talk to your father at some point."

Evelyn scowled. "Why, are you going to make me?"

"It might be-"

"Don't even say that it might be good for me, because it'll be as good for me as swallowing shards of glass."

"That seems a little… extreme."

"Don't care, it's true. That's why you can have every shred of the credit, if you handle the talking. Better yet, he seems to like you a lot, so it makes even more sense, right?"

"Alright, alright, I get it."

She nodded. "Good. Just don't bring it up again and we'll be fine."

"OK. So what are we going to do about getting

information? We're not exactly swimming in options."

Evelyn looked through the file again. "Well, in order to do this the person would need to have access to the foundation's funds. That means they're either in the accounting department, or they're in the executive part."

"Then there's the matter of the alleged shell company," Grant said.

"I can have someone look into that, but I don't think we're going to get very far," she told him. "If they're smart then they'd have a partner open up the company. One that would be difficult to connect to the person on the inside."

"Who's going to look into it?"

"I have my sources."

"Care to share any more than that?"

"There's always David. If he can't find anything then he can always ask someone else. He has a pretty deep web of contacts."

"Seriously?"

Evelyn gave him an amused look. "Why, did you think he was just a butler or something?"

"I thought he was a little bit more than that. But this? I always thought he was just a manager of some sort."

"I think the more appropriate way to put it would be a steward, if we're talking in feudal terms. He's been in charge of the household for as long as I can remember, and that takes a ton of savvy. He's no fool, by any means."

"So he can find something?"

"He'll smile and nod and give you an evasive answer.

But if I ask him he can't refuse the princess."

Grant smiled. "Yes, milady."

"Don't even start with me."

"Next question, then. Who's on the executive board that would do something like this?"

"Well, there's me, Rose and Josie. So those are out."

"I notice you're very quick to eliminate yourself without any evidence," he quipped.

Evelyn shoved him over onto his back and jumped on top of him. "I said don't even start with me, OK?"

He laughed. "OK, OK, I'll stop. I'm guessing none of you need to bother with laundering that kind of money."

"You're guessing right."

"So who else is there?"

"My father, nominally. Obviously he's out. And that's it."

"That's it?"

Evelyn nodded. "And that's it. Control of the foundation is strictly within my family."

"Wait, so does that mean the problem is in accounting?"

"Possibly. But in order to do something like this they'd need to have someone higher up sign off on everything. The accounting department aren't the ones that decide on how to spend the money, they just cut the checks."

"So that means..."

"Could mean that one of the others is doing the laundering, yes."

"Or? I hear an or in there."

"Or more likely, someone else is getting one of them to sign off on everything, and they don't even notice what they're getting into."

Something clicked in his mind. "Wait a minute. You said that their personal assistants were in charge of making everything happen in the day to day operations. Wouldn't that make them the most likely suspects?"

"I think it would. Unfortunately, with no proof..."

"But we can find proof?"

Evelyn looked away. "I'm… not sure I want to rock the boat."

"What does that mean?" he demanded.

"I don't know about Rose and Corey, but Josie seems to be very happy with Michael. He's lasted far longer than most of her other assistants."

"Since when do you care?"

Evelyn scowled at him. "I may not be close to my sisters, but that doesn't mean that I hate them. I'm not just going to pull the rug out from under them out of spite."

"This isn't spite. This is a lot more than that," Grant argued. "And even if she is happy, can you really let him stay around when he's probably only using her for her money?"

"We don't even know if he's responsible."

"When did he arrive?"

"About three years ago."

"See? That flag is about as red as you can possibly get. And are you really going to let them get away with this?"

"Fine. I'll ask David for help, and then we can see what the investigation turns up." She let him sit up.

"And what happens when we find out?" he asked.

"If we find out anything concrete then you report it to my father. After that it's in his hands. We solve the mystery, you get your feather in your cap, and everyone's happy. Well, except for the people going to prison, but they hardly count, right?"

For some reason her response made him frown. "I'm not so sure."

"Not so sure about what? Weren't you the one going on about how they should all be put in prison?"

"Not that. The everyone is happy part," he said. "Can we really assume that's true? Doesn't there have to be more to it?"

Evelyn leaned back on the couch. "Oh, that's right. You wanted to make the foundation bigger, or more efficient, or whatever. That was why you originally asked for it, right? Or was it so you could get in my father's good graces?"

"Of course it was to make it better," he protested.

"OK, so I'll assume that's true for a moment. That means it's up to you to make that happen, right? You really don't need me for that kind of thing."

"I thought-"

"I'm interested in the mystery of where the money's going. Once we find that out then I'm done. I told you that. Everything else is up to you."

"Don't you care?"

Evelyn laughed. "Oh come on, is this some attempt to soften me up by making me see what a difference I've made? Because if it is, you're being very transparent."

"That's not it."

"Then what do you need me for? You're perfectly capable of doing what needs to happen. I don't think you could build an investment firm from the ground up if you didn't have some ability."

"But-"

"But nothing. This is your job. Not mine." She stood up. "I'm going to make a few calls. Get everything we need arranged. Once that's settled we can get to the bottom of this."

"Thanks. Good luck," he said.

Grant watched her go, his mind turning. What had he just stumbled into? Something about the whole thing didn't seem right, and the thought wouldn't leave him. Even with the amount of money being embezzled, it was hardly enough for someone to take this kind of a risk. Grant was fairly well paid, and he imagined the others received similar compensation. Why go through the risk of landing in prison?

Something bigger was happening beneath the surface. Even he could sense it. The question was, what?

Evelyn had been right. Within a few days he had his information, courtesy of David's web of contacts. As he feared, though, there wasn't much, just a few pages of details.

He flipped through them, trying to find something, anything that might give him a clue as to what was going on her who was behind it all. Maybe Evelyn was right. It might be impossible to glean anything from what they could gather on their own. The couldn't exactly hunt down bank accounts and financial statements from an outside company, not without an official investigation.

Grant couldn't find anything useful. Everything in here was just trivia and little else. The company's date of creation, their mailing address, a website…

But then something caught his eye. As Grant read it over he almost dropped the packet in shock. Lost in the middle of the words was the name of the company's owner.

Josephine Arno.

14

"That can't be right," Evelyn said with a frown.

"It's right in here," Grant told her, handing her the document. "Unless there was a pretty big mixup, which I don't believe for a second, she's the owner of the company."

"Let me see that," she said, snatching the paper out of his hands. It only took her a few seconds to read through before she put it down and looked back at him.

"Now do you believe me?"

"That doesn't mean anything."

"What else can it mean? It's as plain as day, right there where we can both see it."

"There has to be more to it. Josie isn't exactly the brightest person when it comes to business, but committing fraud like this isn't like her. And what would be the point? A few hundred thousand dollars? She spends that like it's nothing."

"Are you sure you're not just rationalizing?"

Evelyn shot him a look. "Of course not. There has to be another explanation for this."

"You're rationalizing," he said. "What's more likely? That she doesn't know what's going on, or that she has a hand in it?"

"Then why is this information so readily available? She's not stupid enough to do something that's this easy to discover."

Grant shook his head. "Maybe, but right now it's at least suspicious. Your father needs to know."

Evelyn suddenly grabbed his collar and pulled him closer to her.

"Don't even think about," she said in a low voice.

"About what?"

"About throwing her to the wolves for your own advancement before we even know what's going on. Don't you dare do it. Or..."

Grant looked away. "You have so little faith in me."

"Yeah, well, I'm not taking chances with this. Josie and I may not be close, but she's still my sister, and I'm not going to let you hurt her for your own gain."

He looked back at her. "Think about this for a second. I know you think that she's incapable of doing something like this, but what's the alternative? She's involved somehow."

Evelyn let go and picked the file back up. "Here. Look at the founding date. It's six years ago."

"So?"

"So? Doesn't that seem odd to you? Why would she go through the trouble of founding a front company for this six years ago, only to use it in the last three? And on top of it, for what she'd consider pocket change."

"I think you're grasping at straws."

"And I think you're jumping to conclusions. Are you seriously going to move forward when you're not even sure about this?"

"Who says I'm not?"

Without any warning Evelyn pushed him back onto the couch. Before he knew what was happening she was on top of him, looking down at him with a steely gaze.

"Don't you dare even think about this. There has to be another explanation."

"I think that you're-"

"*Don't.*"

Grant looked back up at her. "You can't protect her forever. If she's involved then the truth is going to come out eventually."

"Yes, it will. But you're not looking for the truth right now, are you? You're just looking for a way to make success so you can get back in my father's good graces, is that right?"

"That's completely unfair," he said.

"But is it untrue?"

"It is," Grant protested. "I know you think that she's not involved. I honestly do. But the evidence doesn't look good right now, and I'm not sure how much that's going to change."

"But it still might. Can you really go through with this knowing it could happen?"

"I never said what I was going to do."

"You said that my father needed to hear about it. And once the word gets back to him, that means opening up a can of worms that's not going to go away. There's no way Josie manages to come out of this unscathed."

"So what else do you want me to do?"

"Hold the information for a bit. Give me some time to look into this. There has to be an explanation."

"But it-"

She put her hand over his mouth. "Just don't. Look yourself and give me more time."

He gently pushed her hand away. "For all we know your father is already aware of this and is just testing me."

"Now who's grasping at straws?"

"Maybe, but it's also a possibility."

"Just… just don't, OK? Just don't. That's an order."

"An order?"

She bit her lip. "I know. I'll make it worth your time."

Grant felt her hand move, and then she suddenly started to tug at his waistband. He grabbed her hand.

"What are you doing?"

"Making this worth your while."

"Seriously? You don't have to seduce me to keep me quiet. I'll keep it to myself for the time being."

Evelyn sat up, an embarrassed look on her face. "Oh."

Grant pushed himself up. "But I have pretty serious

misgivings over this. There's no way she isn't at least partly involved in something like this, and it might not turn out the way you like. But I'll keep quiet for now."

"Thank you."

They sat in silence for a moment.

A thought crossed his mind. "Um, question."

"What?"

"Is your offer still good?"

Grant heard Evelyn sigh as she lay her head against his chest.

"Now you have to keep up your end of the bargain," she said.

"Like I told you, I was planning on doing it anyhow. Why would I suddenly change my mind?"

"Just reminding you."

He ran a hand through her hair. "You can trust me."

"So you say."

"I mean it," he insisted. "I know you said it's hard for you to open yourself up to someone, but you can trust me, at least. Consider my silence proof of that."

"That's just one small step, I'm afraid."

"Then that's one less step I have to take," Grant replied.

Evelyn sat up and met his gaze. "That depends on you staying on the path. Does it matter if you abandon it part way through?"

Now it was his turn to sigh. "So you're still afraid that I'm going to abandon you, is that it? That as soon as a better opportunity presents itself that I'm going to ditch you?"

"That kind of fear just doesn't go away."

"Then is there anything I can do to make it better?"

She looked away. "Just… just understand, OK? Just try to understand."

"I'm not going to abandon you."

"How can I be sure of that?"

"I know you can't. I know that what I'm saying is just words to you now. But it doesn't have to stay that way."

Evelyn frowned. "That's so easy for you to say," she muttered.

Grant suppressed the urge to sigh. Once again he was running into a stone wall and trying to bash it down with his bare hands. No matter how hard he tried or what tactics he used, he was getting nowhere. Would it ever improve? Would she ever be able to open up to him, or was Evelyn always going to keep him at arms length.

But she was trying. It might be hard for her, but Evelyn was at least trying to open up to him. At this point he would take what he could get.

What happens when I open myself to you, only for you to abandon me because you can't handle the prospect of failure? What then?

"What?" Evelyn asked, and Grant realized he must have made some sort of face.

"It's nothing."

"Obviously it's something. Now, spill it."

"Isn't it much better to ask?"

"OK, would you spill it, please," she said, sticking her tongue out at him.

For some reason that made him laugh. "That's a little better."

"Come on, you're just making fun of me now."

"I swear, I'm not doing it on purpose."

"Yeah, I don't believe you. And stop trying to evade the question."

"Do you really have to know?"

"Well, now I do. So what is it?"

Grant hesitated for a moment. "It was something that you said to me."

"What was it?"

He looked away.

"Grant?"

He took a breath and looked back into her eyes. "It was about where you'd be left if you opened yourself up to me and then I abandoned you."

"Oh, that."

"You sound so casual about it."

"Well, what else is there to say? I could lie to you and tell you everything's going to work out perfectly, but what good would that do? Is that what you really want?"

"It isn't, but..."

"But what?"

"It just seems so... dismal, so hopeless. Like you're already convinced it's going to turn out badly."

"So it turns out badly, because it's a self-fulfilling

prophecy?" she asked.

"Well, you could say that."

Evelyn sighed. "Look, I warned you. It's not going to be easy. You're not going to be able to snap your fingers or say a few magic words to make everything alright. It's going to take a lot of time, and I'm not even sure it's going to work out in the end."

"So you're trying not to get my hopes up, is that it?"

"I suppose."

"But is that really the right thing to do?" he asked. "Isn't it better to try and have hope, rather than sealing yourself off and having none? Even if that hope is slim?"

She sighed again. "Do you remember how it felt like when your partners betrayed you?"

"Yeah, I do. It sucked.

"Like being stabbed in the gut, right?"

"I don't know, being stabbed in the gut might have hurt less," Grant said.

"Well, that's where I'm at. You had it happen to you once. What do you think would happen if it happened three, four, five times? Would you really feel like putting yourself out there when you know you're just going to get hurt again?"

Grant didn't respond. Had he felt the same way? He had barely tried to rebuild the shambles of his life over the first year after the betrayal. He thought it was out of grief, out of shock at the treachery of two people that he trusted, but had it also been out of fear of being hurt again? His efforts over the second year lacked the conviction, the fire that had driven him forward.

"I don't doubt that you have good intentions," Evelyn said. "Honestly, most people do, and I know that. But good intentions can only go so far. If they can't actually back them up then what's the point?"

"And the solution is to shield yourself so you can't get hurt like that again," he summarized. "I get it, but you're not completely walled off, are you? There's still a few soft spots in there, right?"

"Maybe a few."

"Your sisters, for one. And not just Miri. You might not want to show it, but deep down you care about the other two."

"I never claimed otherwise," she said sitting up. "But please, don't betray me. Don't sell them out for your own gain."

Grant sat up beside her and put an arm around her. "The same thing happened to me. Why would I inflict it on someone else?"

"Plenty of people do it."

"Not me." He looked out of the windows at the far end of the suite, watching the twilight sweeping over the city. "I made that decision a long time ago."

"Oh?"

"Yeah. I struggled with it a while. My formative years weren't exactly... stable. Had a lot of anger bottled up in there."

"Can't really blame you for that."

"No, but at a certain point I can't blame my behavior on others. I had to fight through a lot to get where I am, but I made a vow to myself. That I'm not going to follow my dad's path. That I'm not going to carry his sins."

"Well, I think you're done a good job of it."

"Thank you."

"And I guess that goes for a lot of the other people that have hurt me," he said. "I guess I just have to keep moving forward, and promise myself that I won't be like them."

Evelyn didn't respond.

"And I know it's not as easy as just saying it," Grant added. "Not even close. I struggle with it a lot. But..."

"No, I get it," she said. "But like I told you, it's hard for me. And expecting anything different at this point just means going in circles."

"I know."

She stood up. "Well, there's too many things that need to be done right now to lie around all evening."

"Do you want help?"

"If you want to give me help then yeah, I'll take it. But I need to get changed first."

"You can use some of my clothing if you want. Not sure how well it'll fit, but at least you can use my t-shirts."

"Do you care which one?"

"Not really."

"OK, I'm going to rinse off first before I get dressed. Want to join me?" she said with a grin.

Grant stood up. "Eh, why not?"

A short while later they were back to work. And once again, Grant's misgivings wouldn't go away.

"Look, I know you're not exactly convinced, but there's something going on here," he said. "At the very least someone forged her signature."

"That's what I'm thinking. Or they got her to sign something that she didn't even bother to check. I'd think that was more likely than Josie pulling off a conspiracy like this for minimal gain."

He groaned and leaned back into the couch. "The problem is that it's nothing more than conjecture at this point. Anyone auditing this is going to think that she's up to something, not that she's unaware and being caught up in it."

"Well, then we just have to find something."

"Yeah, but what? We're going around in circles."

"OK, then let's start over from the beginning. What do we know?"

"That a lot of money has been paid to a consulting firm that's doing busy work at best, and that the firm is owned by your sister."

"Right. And?"

"And that she's in control of the foundation as well, which gives her the opportunity to exploit her position to embezzle money."

"Yes, but then add in more details. How much money is being embezzled?"

"About a hundred thousand dollars each year. Pretty sizable, but not a ton in the grand scheme of things. A lot of money is being thrown away for perfectly legitimate causes as well."

"And that's what bothers me the most. Why would she go through all this trouble for this much money? It's not like she needs it. So why do it?"

"And that's why you suspect someone else is involved," Grant said.

"Right."

"And then the question is what their motive might be. Assuming that she was tricked into this, the question is why? There's only a few people who have access to her for something like this, but what reason would they have to try to pull this off?"

"So you think it was one of her personal assistants?"

"That's the only thing that makes sense. And you said that Michael showed up three years ago. That puts him right in the timeframe for when all the problems started."

"But the company was founded three years prior to that."

"Which again, points back to her being involved," Grant said. "And once again, we're going around in circles."

Evelyn inhaled. "I think we're going to have to ask her about it."

"Are you crazy? If she's involved that'll tip her off. If she isn't but she blabs to the wrong person, it'll tip them off."

"And that takes care of the problem, right? They'd be

idiots if they keep embezzling money when we know what's up. That takes care of them for a while."

"Until they pop up somewhere else."

Evelyn shrugged. "Not my problem. And my father with squash them like a bug if they try it with anything that's actually important to him."

"I don't know…"

"I do. I'm going to ask about it."

"I thought you said that we should keep quiet?"

"I said that *you* should keep quiet."

Grant shook his head. "Fine, fine. We'll do it your way."

15

"You seem tense," Miranda commented as she lazily swam a lap in the pool. "Is there something going on between you and Evie?"

Grant shook his head. "I'd rather not say. But no, there's nothing major going on between us."

He had started getting up much earlier to exercise, and also so he could see Miranda in private. It was good to be able to talk to someone else about what he might be thinking, and she often gave him good insight into Evelyn's personality and actions.

"But there's something going on?"

"Like I said. I'd rather not say."

"Oh, so it's a secret? I can keep secrets."

"Even so."

"Speaking hypothetically, what's troubling you? Completely hypothetical, of course."

Grant sighed. "OK. Hypothetically speaking, say that you know something. You're pretty sure about it, though not completely. But someone else thinks you're wrong, and that there's another explanation."

"You want to know what to do?"

"Yeah, that's where I'm stuck."

"Well, it depends on how much you trust the other person. If you feel confident in their intuition, then you should listen to them. Maybe they have a point."

"But what if holding back and delaying means letting a lot more damage happen?" he asked. "And what if all the evidence points to what you think?"

"Then that's something you're going to have to weigh. Whether you think that you or the other person has the right idea, and whether the other idea has merit."

"But what about if you think they're just rationalizing? Making up an excuse so they don't have to face a hard truth?"

"Again, that's up to your judgement. Whether you trust the other person enough to listen to what they might have to say, even if you think they might be completely off base."

Grant sighed again. "That's what I thought you'd say."

"Well, there's not much else to do. Either you trust them, or you don't."

"That sounds like a very black and white solution to a very grey problem."

"That's a poetic turn of phrase," Miranda commented.

"Well, it was what I could think of. It's an either or

solution, and I'm not sure it's going to work."

"So, what are you doing now? Hypothetically speaking, of course."

"I promised the other person that I'd keep quiet while they explored their theory. Hypothetically."

"Of course. Well, that's about all you can do right now."

"But what if you're certain that they're not going to like what they find. What do you do about it then?" Grant asked.

"Once again, you need to weigh the options. Whether pushing what you believe is the cold, hard truth or letting them explore something else is the right call."

Grant shook his head. "You know, you sound like one of those oracles that give vague prophecies so everyone thinks that they can tell the future. Only they do it so they're never wrong."

Miranda laughed. "I'm not sure if that's a compliment or not, but it's pretty amusing, at least."

"I try," Grant shrugged.

"But to tell you the truth, it's up to you. Whether you can trust her judgement or not."

"I didn't say whether it was a her or him."

He saw Miranda stand up in the shallow end of the pool, a grin on her face. "Hypothetically speaking, I mean."

"Yeah. So that's it, then? It's all about whether I have faith in them?"

"Pretty much."

Grant looked up at the ceiling, thinking. "I don't know whether I can or not. It's not that I think she's wrong-"

"So now we've moved away from hypotheticals into something more concrete?"

"Still hypothetical."

"Of course. Whatever you say."

Grant wasn't sure he wanted to continue the game of hypotheticals, but he also didn't want to out Evelyn. Miranda seemed fairly safe when it came to secrets, but he wasn't sure how far that trust extended. She might try to smooth over the problem, or in the worst case his indiscretion might make its way back to Evelyn. If that happened he would probably never hear the end of it.

"But continue," Miranda told him.

"OK. It's not that I think she's necessarily wrong, it's just that I think she's letting her emotions get the better of her."

"Didn't you say that you thought she was wrong?"

"Well yeah, I think that too, but how far do you think I want to dig that hole for myself?"

"That probably wouldn't go over very well," she agreed.

"So what do I do?"

"Just because a decision is made with emotion doesn't mean it's a bad one," Miranda said. "People are emotional creatures. We often make our decisions in the heat of the moment. That doesn't mean they can't be right."

"Trust their judgment, then?"

"Yes. That would be what I'd do. Of course, that's just a suggestion."

Grant pushed himself up out of the hot tub and

grabbed his towel. "Thanks for the advice."

"My pleasure. And just make sure that Evie stays out of trouble."

"Could you never mention that I asked you about this?" he asked.

Miranda laughed. "Oh, right. Hypothetically."

Grant went back to his room and took a shower, then got dressed and had breakfast. At the moment Evelyn was nowhere to be found, probably still sleeping. If she needed him then he imagined that she'd call.

With nothing else to do Grant went into his study and watched the progress of the stock market, idly watching the graphs and charts go up and down. To him they were little more than a background as he thought about Miranda's advice. It wasn't much, just the same things he had thought when he had relented to Evelyn's request, but at least it gave him a little more confidence that he had made the right call.

He checked his phone several times over the course of the next hour. It wasn't unusual for her to sleep late, but she was usually up by now. Was she just not feeling like being sociable today, or was there something else going-

The sound of his phone vibrating cut into his thoughts. Grant picked it up. As he thought, the message was from Evelyn. He stood up and started to head to his front door as he checked it, expecting to be called to her room.

Instead, it was something completely different.

Please come to the penthouse.

That made him stop in his tracks. Come to the penthouse? Why? And then there was the matter of the first word. Evelyn tended to give orders, not requests. Why was she being so polite right now? He grew more and more alarmed by the second.

Grant sprinted for the elevator, rushing inside and pressing the bottom as fast as possible. Something about this didn't seem right. Something was definitely wrong. But what?

He heard the sound of voices as he exited on the top floor, muffled by the double doors ahead. Grant ran forward, yanked one open and ducked inside the penthouse.

The situation became clear in an instant. Two people stood in the living room, arguing. One was female, the other male. Grant spotted Evelyn's long, blonde hair. The other had his back turned, and Grant couldn't recognize him.

"What's going on?" he demanded, stepping into the room.

Evelyn looked up, an expression of relief spreading across her face. "So you came."

"Of course."

"I thought I told you this was supposed to be between the two of us," the other one said. Grant thought he knew the voice, but he couldn't quite pinpoint it.

"Why the hell would I listen to you?" Evelyn said.

"You wouldn't want anything to happen to your sister, hm?"

Something clicked inside Grant's mind, and his

suspicions were confirmed when the man turned around.

"So. Michael," Grant said. "What's going on?"

"Something that doesn't need to concern you. It's not your business."

His tone touched off a nerve inside of Grant, making him step forward. "I'm making it my business. Now what's going on?"

"He's trying to blackmail me," Evelyn spoke up.

"Such an ugly word."

Grant moved beside Evelyn, keeping an eye on Michael the entire time. "Is that true?"

"Well, I wouldn't put it that way, but-"

"Cut the bullshit. Call it what you want, you want something from me and you're threatening me to make it happen," Evelyn snapped.

A smile crossed Michael's face, a sinister expression almost like a snake sizing up its prey. Grant felt a slight chill go down his spine as he looked on. He definitely had bad intentions in mind.

"You're the cause of all of this. You couldn't just leave it alone. You had to go poking your nose into places where it doesn't belong, instead of being a good little girl and knowing your place."

Evelyn started to respond, but Grant put himself between them and interrupted her.

"Cause of what?"

"Oh, are you the one that decided to let her off her chain?"

"He's the one that's embezzling the money from the foundation," Evelyn spoke up.

Grant glanced over his shoulder at her. "Wait. He *admitted* that to you?"

She looked down at the floor. "There's a little more to it."

"A little more," Michael laughed. "That's what you call it. A little more. There's far more to it than that, and we're going to keep everything the way it is, isn't that right?"

Grant looked him in the eye, feeling a cold fury slowly building inside of himself. He hadn't liked Michael much since he had met him, but this was just making things far, far worse. What was going on?

"Quit speaking in riddles."

"Oh, not one for figuring out a puzzle, hm? I thought you'd like them, since you seem to like to stick your nose into places where it doesn't belong. But maybe she can tell you in a way you can understand."

Grant thought he had seen the worst of Evelyn's glares, but the one she gave Michael in that moment topped them all. Most people would wither in the face it, but Michael stood smirking and apparently oblivious to it.

"He's blackmailing Josie," Evelyn said. "She knows he's embezzling, but he laid a trap for her. For all intents and purposes she's the one moving all the funds, so he can out her anytime he wants to cover his own skin."

"All that for a little bit of money?" Grant asked. "Really?"

Michael shook his head. "You have no vision, do you? No ambition. A few hundred thousand dollars? Do you really think that's enough to spend three years of my life stuck here? She was a way into the Arno Corporation for me, nothing more."

"He's using her as a stepping stone. And he's using the blackmail to try to get into the upper ranks of the company," Evelyn said. Grant could hear the anger in her voice growing by the second.

He felt his own fury swelling as well. "So that's it? You're just using this as blackmail for your own advancement?"

"Call it what you want-"

"But it didn't work, did it?"

Michael glared at him. "What?"

Grant gazed back. "It didn't work, huh? Three years here, and that's three years you've been a personal assistant and nothing more. What happened to your grand scheme?"

Michael clenched his fists by his sides. "That's right. The eldest daughter to the leader of the Arno Corporation, and she's completely useless. What has she accomplished? What can she do? I spend all this time and effort, and she's worthless."

"Watch your tone," Evelyn said in a low voice. Grant could feel the tension in the room start to reach a breaking point.

"So we're going to keep it this way, hm? I wonder what your father would say about the embarrassment when one of his own daughters is caught stealing from a charity, hm? What a scandal that would be."

"Shut up."

"No, that's what you're going to do. You're going to be a good girl, go back to your life and not say a damn thing about this. Otherwise your sister's going to be spending quite a few years inside a prison cell, isn't that right?"

"You're going into the cell right beside her."

Michael laughed. "Who, me? I'm just the poor assistant that did all the gopher work, not even realizing what I was doing. I admit, I should have been a bit more watchful, but you really can't blame me for this." He looked at Grant with a malicious grin. "Right?"

"Whatever," Grant muttered, though his statement cut deep.

Evelyn started to walk away. "Enjoy this for the time being. You'll-"

Michael reached out and grabbed her by the wrist. "I didn't tell you that you could leave. Now, let's make this very clear-"

Evelyn lashed out, catching him in the side of his face with her ring. Michael staggered back for a moment, then lunged forward and slapped her with the back of his hand, throwing her to the ground.

"Now," he said as he stood over her. "You're going-"

The rest of his words came out as a gurgle. Grant grabbed him by the throat with one hand and slammed him against the wall.

"Touch her again and I'll kill you," he said, his voice deceptively calm. He could feel his rage boiling under the surface, barely held in check.

Grant held his grasp for another second to make his point, then stepped back and turned away.

"Oh, so you're going to kill me, is that it?" Michael taunted him. "You won't do it. Or maybe shouldn't say that. Maybe you want to share a cell with your old man, is that right?"

That was it. Grant whirled around and lunged at him, preparing to mash his face into a bloody pulp. But he stumbled as something grabbed his wrist, and an arm wrapped around his chest…

"He's not worth it," Evelyn said in his ear. "Let's go."

Grant gave Michael one last glare before following her out of the penthouse.

"Are you OK?" Grant asked as the elevator doors closed.

"Physically? Yeah, I'm fine. He surprised me, that's all."

"Are you sure?"

"Yeah. Although you surprised me back there too. I honestly thought you were going to kill him if I didn't stop you," she said with a hint of a smile.

Grant looked away. "I probably would have. You know why."

"Well, then I'm glad I stopped you. We can't have something like that to deal with at this point."

"I know."

"But thank you for looking out for me anyhow."

Grant glanced back at her. "So what are we going to do?"

Evelyn sighed. "I don't know. I really don't. He outright admitted his guilt, but he's holding all of the cards now. If we do this wrong then Josie's going down with him. Or she's going to be the only one taking the fall."

"There has to be something we can do."

"He's gloating. That probably means he covered his tracks pretty well, otherwise why bother giving us all that information? He has to have something else up his sleeve."

"Or maybe he's cocky and is just gloating for the sake of it."

She shook her head. "Maybe, but we can't take chances with that. I'd assume the worst."

"So what do you want to do about it? We can't just let this go."

"No, but if we do this wrong it could turn out very badly. If it looks like he's going to be cornered then I'd be willing to bet he'll try to take as many people down with him as he can."

Grant nodded. "That sounds pretty likely."

"So I think we need to look into this more. Very discretely."

"What's your plan of attack?"

"The company," she shrugged. "I'm still having a hard time believing that he could have plan this out three years in advance."

"Well, what other explanation is there?"

"I didn't ask about it when I talked to Josie, but I think we need to figure out how it was founded. Her signature was on it, but maybe it was forged. Or maybe it was something that she started and completely forgot about."

"If that second one is true...," Grant mused aloud, then trailed off.

"What?"

"If the second one is, true, then that might explain the difference in dates," he said. "He might have just found a relatively defunct company out of chance and then just took the opportunity to exploit it."

"You're thinking pretty clearly, for what just happened a few minutes ago," Evelyn commented. "Almost like you're able to forget about it. That's a good skill."

"I haven't forgotten about it."

"But you're still thinking clearly for how enraged you were," she said.

The elevator opened up at their floor.

"Well, I want to throw him off the top of the tower, but you won't let me," Grant said. "Since I can't do that, finding a way to bust him then grinding his face in the dirt while it happens sounds like the next best thing."

"But you still want to?"

"Oh yeah. Probably beat him into a pulp before I do it too."

Evelyn giggled for a moment. "I feel so flattered."

Grant looked over at her. "Are you really OK?"

"Well, I'm not happy about it, but he really didn't hurt me. Nothing I can't handle. Though I feel pretty dirty right now."

"Are you sure?"

"You're getting very protective, all of a sudden."

"I just loathe people like him," Grant said. "After watching my father... I'm not letting something like that happen again if I have the power to stop it."

"You're so noble."

Grant thought he heard a hint of sarcasm in her voice and scowled. "I'm not trying to be a white knight. I just hate people like that and want to make them pay."

"Oh, so you're an avenger and not a rescuer?" Evelyn said. She waved her ring hand in front of the lock.

"I really don't care about distinctions at this point."

"Fair enough. Well, like I said, I feel dirty after spending all that time speaking with him. So I'm going to go wash off. Meet me back here in about an hour?"

"For a moment I thought that you were going to make me come with you to wash you off."

Evelyn pursed her lips. "That didn't go so well last time, so I'm not going to make you do that. Unless you want to?"

"If you want me along I'll go," Grant told her. "Right now I feel pretty dirty as well."

That made her smile as she took his hand. "OK then, maybe I can return the favor. Come on."

16

They made very little progress over the next few weeks. After hours and hours upon digging they still had nothing to show for it. Michael's scheme seemed to be well-planned. All signs pointed back to Josephine as the culprit. They only thing they had to implicate him was an admission of guilt, and that wasn't going to hold up against the mountain of evidence pointing toward her.

Grant thought about asking Robert for help several times, but he didn't want to bring it up to Evelyn. This was already hard enough for her, and bringing in her father would probably only make things worse. Besides, there was no guarantee that he would take their side. Josephine might be his daughter, but he might be inclined to believe the evidence instead.

He could only feel his frustration growing by the second. Once again he was being confronted by fraud and deception, manipulated by someone for their own gain. And like the situation with his former partners, Grant had no control over anything. He couldn't fight back, could hardly keep up with all the developments happening around him.

And then there was Evelyn. In some ways her presence made this even harder. At least during his previous trials he had been the only one affected by the changes. But this situation was dragging her through the muck, confronting her with the very real possibility that her sister was about to suffer an awful fate.

Blood was thicker than water, it turned out. Her initial statements might have made him thought she despised her older siblings, but clearly she did care for their well-being, at least. And even if there was tension between them, they were really the only close relationships she had in this world. Those three, and him.

Grant flopped back onto the couch and stared at the ceiling, wondering about that. Could they really be considered a close relationship at this point, or were they just acting one out, playing their parts for the time being until something else pulled them away from each other?

Do you love me?

He covered his eyes with his arm. "Why did you have to ask me that?" he muttered to himself.

The question might have been innocent enough, but it continued to haunt him. Did he really love her, or was this a passing fancy? Was he just trying to be the noble white knight like she suspected, riding in to save the princess? And was she right to worry that he would abandon her when the path ahead became difficult?

And then there was Michael. Him. Grant felt a sense of loathing in the pit of his stomach as he thought about him. Michael might be all of Evelyn's worst nightmares come to fruition: domineering, ambitious to the point of being ravenous, willing to use people as pawns to get what he wanted, and devious.

Was he any different? Grant certainly believed so, but was Michael always this way? Had he started out just like him and then slowly became twisted into the monster he had become today? Was he headed down the same path? Both of them had come here to feed their ambitions, to further their prestige and their careers. The only difference was that he had caught the eye of their benefactor, while Michael languished behind the scenes.

Why didn't you chose something different when you failed at your investment firm? Why did I have to come drag you out of that pit?

No matter how hard he tried to forget them, Evelyn's words still haunted him, and they became even worse when he looked at Michael. It wasn't that he was completely loathsome, or that Grant hated his guts and wanted to make him pay for hurting Evelyn. No, it was the fact that, despite their differences, Grant might be looking at himself in a few years if he continued down this path.

He didn't think it would ever get that bad, but…

Grant heard his phone go off, and for a moment he

thought he had received a text message. But then the phone went off again, and he grabbed for it. Someone was calling.

"Hello?"

"Are you awake?" Evelyn asked on the other end of the line.

"It's two in the afternoon. Of course I'm awake."

"Well, maybe you were taking a nap or something."

"I'm not a cat."

"No, you're not. Puppy." Grant could almost hear the smile on the other end of the line.

"So what do you want?"

"There's something I want to do this evening," she said.

"What's that?"

"Go out for dinner."

"That's it?" Grant asked, confused. He didn't know why she would need to call him for that. Normally she'd just message him, or more likely show up at his door and drag him out.

"Of course there's more. We're going to have someone else with us. Out in the city, away from prying eyes."

"Who's that?"

"You remember David, right?"

"What do you mean, do I remember David? Of course I do."

"Just checking. Anyhow, he's going to be with us tonight."

Grant suspected he knew why. "Care to give any more details, or do you not want to take the chance of spilling any secrets?"

"What, like you think that he has our rooms bugged? There's no way he could do it, and even if he could I doubt he's stupid enough to try. That's just more prison time."

"He'll blackmail us to get out of it."

"Of course, but even if he does he still goes to prison, and I'm pretty sure he doesn't want to spend a few years there."

"So, back to what we were talking about. Anything you want to enlighten me about before we go to dinner?"

"Not really. I'm sure you'll figure it out."

"I have some ideas."

"And they'll probably be correct, or at least close to the mark. Oh, and dress well. We're not going to a fast food joint."

"Oh really? I half suspected that we were," Grant said with a smile.

"Just for that I'm not ordering anything for you the next time I get takeout," she replied. "Be ready to go at six."

"Got it. I'll see you then."

Grant hung up and leaned back into the couch, thinking. With such little progress he imagined Evelyn was extremely frustrated. But with the news they were meeting with David outside of the tower, he believed his suspicions were confirmed. She was done playing around. Now she was going to bring down the full force of her wrath down on Michael. Surrender might be the best option for him at this point. If he did anything to hurt Josie then Evelyn would smash him.

The thought made him grin, for some reason. It was a good thing that he despised Michael. Otherwise, he might actually feel sorry for him.

"Mr. Adams, it's been too long," David greeted him, extending his hand.

"Far too long," Grant agreed, shaking his hand. "Thank you for all your help."

"Think nothing of it. They're just part of my duties, after all."

"Well, thank you for coming anyhow," Evelyn told him, giving him a hug. "I wish it could be for something a lot more pleasant."

"Yes, that is unfortunate. It's a pity that Miss Josephine was unable to pick out a good assistant like you were."

"Thank you," Grant said with a smile.

"Luck of the draw, I guess," Evelyn shrugged.

"Oh, so you're a broken clock now?"

David laughed. "Well, I think that proves it. Too many of the others were unwilling to talk back to you. Well, except Patrick, but-"

"Let's not talk about that," she interrupted him.

"Which one was that?"

"Seventy five."

"Huh? Oh. Ohh."

"Remember now?"

"Yeah. Thanks."

"Well, you're the one who asked."

"And my point is only proven further," David said, taking a seat at the table. "I imagine that you want to wait a bit before we start on business, am I correct?"

"Yes. No use talking about these kind of things on an empty stomach," Evelyn agreed.

"Is this a safe place to talk?" Grant asked.

David smiled at him. "Of course. We're in a private room. And as for anyone listening in, that won't be a problem. I doubt our arrogant friend has anyone willing to do his dirty work in here. Certain, in fact."

"He's a part-owner of the restaurant," Evelyn said.

"That answers my question, then."

They conversed over dinner, servings of bread, salad and a pasta dish with seafood in a white wine sauce. Grant had to make sure not to stuff himself. He wanted to be attentive for this conversation.

The server offered them wine. Evelyn declined for obvious reasons, and Grant followed her example. He noticed that David waved the server away as well.

"So you're refusing alcohol to show solidarity with the young miss as well, eh?" David said. "Good, very good."

Grant shrugged. In his mind it wasn't much of a loss, and he didn't want to do anything to make her feel uncomfortable. Evelyn might say she was fine with him drinking, but he wondered if that was actually the case. Better to err on the side of caution, in his mind.

Once the servers cleared away the dishes they got

down to business.

"So you're looking for more information on Mr. Grayson?"

"That's correct," Evelyn told him. "Right now he has a stranglehold on the available information. He has all the cards. But there has to be something missing some sort of opening we can exploit."

"I see. And you want to find it in the most circumspect way possible."

"Yes. I know I've been telling you that, but all the information I've been getting has been leading to dead ends. I need you to call in a few favors."

"Oh?"

"Some of the more valuable ones."

David sat back in his chair and crossed his fingers. "That may be a bit of an issue. People are going to want to know why they're asking around and doing certain things."

"Can you avoid giving them anything other than the basics they need?"

"I can certainly try, but there's no guarantee that they'll be willing to cooperate. I'm owed a few favors, but that doesn't mean I can dictate my will to them. They'll need to have some reason, especially if they have to deal in some of the more dubious aspects of their fields."

"Um, question?" Grant asked.

"Yes?"

"What kind of contacts are we talking about, exactly?"

"Very well placed ones," Evelyn told him.

David nodded. "Friends I have in the government, in various large businesses, in law enforcement. All of them have certain skills that they can bring to the table. And in exchange I can use my own skills to help them."

"Is this legal?"

David laughed. "Of course it is. It might skirt the bounds of ethics, somewhat, but we're not so foolish as to do something illegal. We'll keep our hands clean, at the very least."

"I want to look into the bank accounts," Evelyn said.

"Getting access to them isn't going to be easy. There's a lot of legal red tape to overcome. This is the kind of thing you'll need a warrant for."

"So it's a no go?" Grant asked.

"In this case, probably. Not without crossing over legal lines that my friends won't."

"Then is there some way we can convince them to investigate it legally? Being circumspect, of course."

"That might be difficult."

"Maybe not," Evelyn spoke up. "Don't you have friends in federal law enforcement?"

"I do, but they're busy people. This would normally be something for a more local investigation, but I'm not sure that we could keep that quiet."

Evelyn pulled something out of her purse. "I think this says differently. It's the company's papers and information."

"What about it?" Grant asked.

"Simple. The company is based out of state, in

Wilmington, Delaware. I imagine that their bank accounts are going to be connected there somewhere as well. That means there's fraud being committed over state lines. And since there's probably extortion going on as well..."

"That would put it within Immigration and Customs' jurisdiction," Grant finished. "I guess that's the opening."

"Not necessarily," David said. "It might seem that way, but there needs to be something more concrete. Otherwise we may be simply pointing them in the direction of Miss Josephine."

"Well, how about this?"

Grant watched Evelyn pulled out her phone and set it on the table. She pressed a button, and audio began to fill the room.

"I thought I told you this was supposed to be between the two of us."

"Why the hell would I listen to you?"

"You wouldn't want anything to happen to your sister, hm?"

"So. Michael. What's going on?"

"Something that doesn't need to concern you. It's not your business."

Evelyn pressed the screen and stopped the audio. "It goes on, but you get the idea."

"Wait, you recorded the entire conversation?"

"I did, yes."

"When did you have time to do that?"

"I hid my phone. In, um, a safe spot."

A thought entered his mind. "Wait, does that mean there's audio proof of him assaulting you?"

"Yeah. Just like there's audio proof of you threatening to kill him. I know they're not exactly equal offenses, but I think we should have something more before we start slinging accusations around. So you don't get in trouble, of course."

"But this is proof..."

"Not quite," David said. "The recording may or may not be admissible during a legal proceeding. It all depends on whether they can establish who's speaking. And the audio quality isn't the best."

"Is that why you didn't immediately use it?"

"That is," Evelyn nodded. "But admissible or not, that's at least something to start with. I imagine some of your friends would be very interested in this kind of recording."

"I think they would," David said with a smile. "And I think that this puts more than enough doubt on Miss Josephine's role in all of this to keep her out of trouble for the time being. They'll have questions, to be sure, but nothing too bad."

"Does this solve our problem then?" Grant asked.

Evelyn shook her head. "No. We can't let him get wind of this, because there's no telling what he'll do once he's cornered."

"I'll increase security measures, just in case. I don't want him to harm anyone," David told them.

"Won't that tip him off?" Grant inquired.

"They won't be apparent. Just putting our people on alert so they can deal with the situation."

Evelyn looked at him. "Can you defend yourself?"

Grant shrugged. "Sure."

"I mean, if he tries to bust your door down with a fire axe can you defend yourself?"

"Isn't that a little extreme?"

"You didn't answer my question."

"I guess? What about you?"

"I have a handgun in my room. If he tries anything then I'm emptying the entire magazine into him."

"Why am I not surprised?"

"I can secure some form of protection for you," David said.

Grant shook his head. "Thank you, but I'll be fine."

"I'll give this to you to make sure it's not stolen," Evelyn said, handing over her phone to David.

"I'll be sure to make a copy, just in case, and then I'll send this through the appropriate channels. And I'll make sure that you'll have another phone sent to you."

"Make sure you check the message when I send you my new phone number," Evelyn said.

"Won't that also possibly tip them off?" Grant asked. "He might start wondering why you suddenly changed your phone number."

"How is he going to find out?"

"Do you really want to take a chance with that?" Grant asked. He knew he was being paranoid, but in this situation it might be warranted.

"Then I'll just pretend I'm ignoring messages from everyone else. Simple enough."

She might think so, but Grant had a feeling they weren't out of the woods yet. Too many things could go wrong, and any one of them could be devastating. It might seem like they had the upper hand now, but that all depended on their foe. Michael might have yet another trick up his sleeve.

"I'm not going to be sorry to see him go," Evelyn said the next morning. "He was always a little too arrogant for his own good. Now we know why."

"Agreed," Grant said. "I got that sense the first time I met him. Can't say I'll be sorry to see him put away either."

"Hah, I'll bet," Evelyn replied with a grin. "I should have let you kill him, but that means a bunch of other problems for you, and we don't want that, do we?"

"What, can't make him have an accident? Fall down a dozen flights of stairs or something?"

She laughed. "You're getting into pretty dark territory there."

"Well, he hasn't exactly endeared himself to me. And slapping you pretty much destroyed any chance of being kind to him."

"Naturally."

Grant frowned for a moment. "One thing. I'm still not sure why he didn't check you for a recorder."

"He did. And he found one."

"Wait, what?"

"I had a voice recorder with me. An actual voice recorder, not my phone. I was hoping to use that, since the audio would be clearer, but I suspected he might search me."

"How did he find it?"

"Searching, of course. Grabbed it out of my pocket."

"Wait, so he just felt you up to find it?" Grant asked, feeling the anger rising in him.

Evelyn laughed. "Oh, jealous?"

"That's not funny."

"Well, he did search me. Not invasively or anything. I didn't exactly hide the recorder in the most secure spot."

"But then-"

"The other one?" she asked. Evelyn tapped between her breasts. "He didn't bother to search here. Why would he? He already had the tape recorder in hand."

"Still..."

Evelyn laughed. "What, are you going to throw him off of the building for touching me?"

"The thought's crossing my mind, yeah."

"Don't worry about it."

Grant shook his head. "But-"

"No buts about it. It's fine."

"Is that really true?"

"Of course. All part of the plan."

Grant looked at her. "Are you just saying that to make it seem better?"

Evelyn shook her head. "No. Why would I bother?"

"Well..."

"You know what? Try to hit me."

"What?"

"Take a swing at me and try to hit me."

"Why?"

Evelyn gave him a frustrated look. "Just do it."

Grant hesitated for a moment, then stepped forward and swung a hand at her.

Evelyn slapped it aside and gave him another frustrated look. "I said try to hit me."

"I did."

"No you didn't."

"Fine then," Grant said, swinging harder this time.

He braced himself, trying to hold back to cushion the blow...

But the motion of his arm suddenly stopped, and then he was on the ground. He tried to move, but then he realized Evelyn had him in some sort of arm-bar.

"Still slow, but you were going to take all day otherwise."

"Wait, you can fight?"

"Yeah. Not extremely well, but I can catch people by surprise," Evelyn said as she let him up. "I could have easily done it to him."

"Then why didn't you?"

"To give him the illusion that he's in control. To make him think I'm weaker than I really am."

Grant looked at her. "So that was all just an act?"

Evelyn gazed back at him with a cold edge in her eyes. "Yes. He may think he's in control, but he's wrong. Very wrong. He's only in control so long as I *let* him. When I change my mind there's going to be hell to pay."

Grant looked away, feeling an involuntary shiver go down his spine. Her ability to dominate was showing again. He had seen plenty of it, but it always had a playful side to it. In contrast, Michael was about to feel the edge of its cold, hard fury. Grant almost felt a bit of pity for him. Almost.

"Oh," Evelyn said, interrupting his thoughts. "You're sleeping in my room from now on until we take care of this problem."

"Why?"

"Because you won't protect yourself, so I'm going to have to do it for you."

"Is that really-"

"That's not a request."

Grant shrugged. "Fine then."

"You sound so unhappy about it," Evelyn said with a smile.

It wasn't the request that bothered him, it was what it implied. Evelyn may have said it casually, but ordering him to do so meant she was seriously worried about what Michael might do if he was trapped.

But then, maybe that was just him being paranoid.

17

Grant rolled over as he heard the sound of an alarm going off. It took him another second to determine where the noise was coming from. It was Evelyn's phone going off on the nightstand, too far out of reach for him.

He didn't have to, though. Apparently Evelyn was expecting some sort of message or call, because she grabbed it almost immediately.

"Hello?" She paused. "I see. Any time is fine. Just make sure that you're discrete."

"What was that about?" Grant asked after she hung up.

"Well, looks like we have a bit of a breakthrough," she said. "David is coming up to give us information."

"That was fast."

"Well, that's what happens when you can access anything and everything you want. Let's just hope that he has some good news to go along with it."

Grant looked up at the clock. "Why do it in the middle of the night, though?"

"Because I don't want to tip him off," Evelyn explained. "I don't think he's watching this floor or anything, but you never know. I'd rather play it safe."

"Isn't that going to be suspicious, if he somehow installed a camera or something on this floor? He's going to be really curious why your head of house is showing up at your door in the middle of the night."

"He has to see it first, and that means checking footage. If he even has the ability to do that. This is probably not even necessary, but I think we should stay safe, just in case."

Grant pushed himself up out of bed with a groan and moved to get dressed.

"You don't need to be there if you want to go back to sleep," Evelyn told him.

"The hell I don't. You really think I'm just going back to sleep and ignoring this?"

She smiled. "Didn't think so, but I felt like I had to offer it, at least."

"It's not like I have to get up for work tomorrow. Actually, I'm technically doing work right now."

"Maybe I'll wake you up early."

"That would require *you* to get up early as well, so I'm pretty sure that you're not going to do it."

Grant quickly dressed himself in a pair of jeans and a t-shirt, then looked back at Evelyn. "I'll go let him in, if you don't mind."

"Sounds good," she replied, her voice muffled as she pulled a sweater over her head.

Grant made his way down out of the loft and headed toward the front door, wondering what kind of information David might have for them. If it was from his ICE contacts then it had only taken a couple of weeks go gather the data, which surprised him. He thought it would have taken several months at least, possibly more.

And then there was the question of what the information would mean. Grant imagined that they'd have some sort of access to the other side of the equation, able to know where the money was going. But would that only implicate Michael, or would it drag down others with him? Grant remembered how long and difficult the exoneration process had been, even when he had done nothing wrong.

If things didn't line up perfectly then this could end up very messy, probably in a way that Evelyn didn't want. Even if Josie was innocent it could take months or years to clear her name, and her name would probably be dragged through the mud in the process. Tabloids and gossip sites would certainly to it to make headlines.

He heard the doorbell ring as he stepped into the hallway and hurried to open the door.

"Good evening," David greeted him. He quickly entered the suite and shut the door behind him. "Is the young miss-"

"I'm ready," Grant heard her say from the end of the hall. "What do you have for us?"

"Information, of course. Confidential information that can never leave this room. This is all part of an official investigation, and if word got out it would probably compromise the whole thing."

"So how did you get ahold of it?" Grant asked, following him into the living room. "Isn't this the type of thing to get someone fired or put in prison if it leaks?"

"Yes, it is. But that only happens if people find out it actually leaked. And everyone has the price they're willing sell at. You just need to fulfill their obligations."

"At any rate, we're not going to cause problems," Evelyn said. "I just want the information so we can have an idea of what's going on and how to counter his moves. We'll leave the rest of it up to law enforcement to take care of."

"Provided we want them to do that," Grant cautioned.

She shrugged. "Well, at this point we can't exactly put the genie back in the bottle..."

Grant sat down on the couch in silence. That was a point he hadn't considered much. Bringing the problem to the attention of a government agency gave them far more information to work with, but it also meant that they couldn't just make the problem go away. If there was serious criminal activity going on then they weren't just going to ignore it.

"Was that the plan?" he asked.

Evelyn sighed. "Not really, but we were running out of choices. Either we did nothing and it would be discovered eventually, or we charged right in and he burned everything to the ground around her. This at least gives Josie a fighting chance. I think."

Grant nodded. He could see her point, but they hadn't even seen the information yet. For all they knew it could just point to her guilt.

David sat down in a chair and placed his briefcase on the table, then opened it up. Grant saw him grab a few sheets that looked like they came off from a legal pad. A closer glance revealed they were handwritten notes, not typed like he had expected.

"Is there a reason they didn't type them?" he asked.

"They didn't want to take any chances with the metadata, or so I was told," David informed him. "And I'm willing to accommodate them, since they're putting themselves at risk. Once again, none of the information I'm going to share with you can leave this room."

"Of course," Evelyn said. "Now what do you have for us?"

He handed over one of the sheets of paper. "Financial statements for the company. As you're well aware the money goes from the foundation into the consulting firm's account in Delaware. But after that it gets very interesting indeed."

Evelyn read through the paper. "Wait, an account in the Cayman Islands?"

Grant looked at her. "Seriously?"

"According to the ICE investigation, yes."

Grant turned to David. "Why would he do that? Is he stupid enough to think he can actually hide his money there? Does he not know the difference between a tax neutral location and a somewhere with bank secrecy?"

"Perhaps he's been reading too many crime novels," David said with a wry smile.

"Or maybe this is all part of his plan," Evelyn said. "I notice that Josie's name is on the account."

"That's correct."

"Then this might make more sense if he's actually trying to frame her."

Grant frowned. "Wait, so you think he's trying to get caught?"

"Think about it for a second. The pop culture stereotype is that you can hide money in the Cayman Islands, even though that's not even remotely true. What better way to frame the ditzy heiress than to make her follow that stereotype?"

"So if there's ever an investigation then the trail leads right back to her," Grant summarized. "And it makes it look like she was attempting to cover her tracks, even though it was done clumsily."

"Exactly. Actually, I'm pretty glad that you didn't think that nonsense was true."

Grant shrugged. "I was an investment broker. I dealt with that kind of thing all the time, including all the idiots that thought I could actually help them dodge taxes by investing there."

"And they thought you were lying to them when you said you couldn't, I'm guessing," Evelyn said with a smirk.

"Yeah. Fun times."

"Unfortunately for your theory, all evidence points to her being the culprit," David said.

Evelyn nodded. "Yeah. I'm willing to bet that he's going to point to her if he's caught. Claim that she forced him into doing everything. And that kind of accusation is going to be pretty hard to counter without good evidence to refute it."

"What about the recording?" Grant asked.

"That will help, especially since you helped to establish that you were talking to Michael. Whether it will be enough to take away all the blame from Ms. Arno remains to be seen. And there's some other issues on the recording. The potential assault, for one, and your threats. They could land you in trouble, if he tries to sue you."

"I'll risk it," Grant shrugged.

"Yeah you will," Evelyn agreed. "If he tries anything I'll make sure to back you. That's if my father doesn't let his own army of lawyers loose on him for you."

"That's pretty comforting, actually. But is the recording going to be enough to clear her name?"

"That will be the trouble," David said. "It may all come down to a court decision, and there's no guarantee that it will turn out the way you want. And even if it does it will bring all manner of unwanted publicity."

Grant nodded. He had seen more than his fair share of media attention during his trials, and that had been as barely notable person until the scandal broke. He had no idea what kind of circus would surround the daughter of one of the most powerful businessmen in the world.

"We may have to take that risk," Evelyn said. "I don't want her to be around him any longer than she has to be. If that means there has to be a rough patch..."

Grant looked over at her. "Are you sure? This might be a little more than a rough patch."

"I still don't know. But this is out of my hands now too. I'm guessing that ICE isn't just going to let something like this slide."

"I can try to get them to hold off for a bit," David said, "but it's impossible to keep it from happening at some point."

She nodded. "I understand. Is there anything else?"

"Nothing else." David stood up. "If I hear anything else I'll make sure to let you know."

They sat in silence for a few minutes after David exited the suite. Grant remained unsure whether to say anything or not. He didn't envy Evelyn's position, at the very least. She could report the corruption going on underneath their noses, but that risked putting her sister in the crosshairs of a government investigation. Or, she could stay silent, knowing the status quo couldn't last forever.

And then there was his choice. He could sit by and do nothing for now, bowing to Evelyn's decision. But he had also been tasked with investigating the foundation by Robert Arno himself. Could he just ignore that for now? On the other side, could he sell out Josephine for his own gain, and by extension sell out Evelyn as well?

"What do you think?"

Grant snapped back to reality. "What?"

"What do you think I should do?" Evelyn asked. She pushed herself up out of her seat and began pacing back and forth.

"What do *you* think that you should do?"

"I'm not sure. That's why I'm asking you."

Grant thought about it for a minute. "Honestly, I really don't envy you. That's a pretty tough decision."

"That's not an answer. Are you just stalling for time?"

"No." He paused for a moment. "It's going to happen eventually. Once you got the government involved that ended any possibility that you could just sweep this under the rug. So you might as well do it on your own terms."

"So you think that we should go for it as soon as possible, huh? That we shouldn't try to delay them at all?"

"I think that's your decision. But you can't stop it forever. I guess the only thing you can do right now is to minimize the damage," Grant said.

Evelyn stopped pacing and flopped down on the couch beside him. "I think I just made the wrong decision," she said.

"Why?"

"Because there's no way this turns out well, and there's no way to stop it. Either I sell out my sister, or I let this continue knowing she's going to get caught in the crossfire sooner or later."

"She at least has a fighting chance because you chose to

do something about it," Grant said, trying to encourage her.

"That's really not very comforting."

He sighed. "I know. There's really nothing you can do about it. Unless..."

"Don't even think about it."

"Huh?"

She looked him in the eye. "You're thinking about reporting this to my father, right? Taking the decision out of my hands and making yourself the villain, right?"

"Where did that come from?"

"Don't deny it, that kind of thought crossed your mind. Or maybe you were just going to sell her out for your own personal gain."

"OK, they both might have crossed my mind," he admitted. "The first one a lot more seriously than the second. I'm not selling Josie out."

"You'd better not, otherwise there's going to be hell to pay. I'll make sure of it. She's been through too much."

"I know. And I'm not going to make it worse. There's no way I'm going to be anything like him," he said, clenching a fist at the thought.

"Michael?"

"Yeah, I guess."

"So we're going to have to go through with this," Evelyn said. "And no matter what she's going to come under a lot of scrutiny. I'm not sure that she'll be able to handle that kind of pressure."

"She'll make it."

"And if she can't? I'm honestly really worried about her."

Grant thought for a moment. "You know, this might be far easier on her if she cooperated with the investigation from the beginning," he said. "If she is innocent then she could probably give some more insight on how he's doing the embezzlement."

"Provided she cooperates," Evelyn said. "I don't know how much of a hold he has over her, and that might be difficult for her to break."

"We can help."

"Of course we will. But that doesn't mean it'll work."

Grant couldn't exactly disagree. He had seen the ugly side of an abusive relationship firsthand, and he knew how hard it could be for someone to escape from its clutches. But still…

"I can't just sit here and let him abuse her," Grant said. "I don't know what he's doing to her, but considering how he acted toward you when no one else was watching I don't think it's very pleasant."

"I don't think so either," Evelyn agreed. "And I can't just leave Josie to the wolves either. But we're going to have to be careful. We don't want to tip him off. Otherwise, who knows what he'll try to do."

"Do you think he'll get violent if he'd cornered?"

"I don't know. But I don't want to take that chance, either. If he does I want her as far away from him as possible. If we do this, that is."

"If?"

Evelyn groaned. "I don't know, I still can't decide what to do. There's too much going on here. Too many things that could turn out badly if I choose the wrong path."

Grant stood and pulled her up beside him. "It's going to be the same in the morning. Why don't you at least sleep on it to give yourself a little more time to think?"

"Like I'm going to be able to do that now."

"Well, at least try," he said, leading her back up into the loft. That was the only advice he could offer at this point. The rest was completely in her hands.

Sun streamed through the windows as Grant awoke and sat up, taking in the morning light.

"Finally awake?"

He looked over at Evelyn. "Did you sleep at all?"

"For an hour here and there, but it wasn't easy. I was awake for a lot of it."

"So..."

"So did I make a decision? Is that what you're asking?"

"I guess that was what I was going to ask," he replied.

Evelyn shook her head. "I kept going back and forth a lot. I know it's going to happen eventually, but I don't want to sell out my own sister. And..."

"Do you mind if I say something?"

"Go ahead."

"Pushing the investigation ahead right now might not be the right decision. It might be. I don't know. But..."

"But what?"

Grant took a breath before responding. "Don't sit by and do nothing and regret it later. If you're going to be wrong, I think it's better to be wrong trying to move forward."

Grant saw her smile.

"Ever the romantic, huh?"

"I just think that's the best idea," he shrugged. "Whether you take the advice is another thing entirely."

"I know. But thank you anyhow." She reached for her phone on the nightstand and took a deep breath. "I guess this is it. Cross your fingers."

Grant watched her dial a number, guessing that she was probably contacting David to inform him of the decision. But the words that came out of her lips were something entirely different.

"Hello, Rose? I need your help."

18

"This feels like an intervention," Grant quietly said to Evelyn as they sat in Rose's living room.

"Well it pretty much is one," she replied. "If everything goes well, that is."

Grant nodded, looking around the room to try to kill some time. This was the first time he had been inside Rose's room, and the décor surprised him a bit. It all looked relatively homey, all things considered, with wood paneling along the walls and plush red carpets on the floors.

"So we're clear on this?" Rose asked as she sat down in a chair. "We're not letting her out of this room, no matter what happens."

"Hopefully we'll be able to convince her to cooperate," Miranda added.

"If not then we're still keeping her here while they take care of the problem. I'm not letting her anywhere near him."

Evelyn nodded. "Agreed."

Grant had been slightly taken aback by the mood in the room. The other three were focused and serious, in contrast to their usual moods. He could hardly blame them, though. They were attempting to protect their sister whatever way they could."

"You took care of the arrangements, right?" Rose asked him.

Grant nodded. "I did. David confirmed it with his contacts. He may have embellished it a little as well, but it got the results we need. They're going to make the arrest today."

"What did you do?" Miranda asked.

"I told David to tell his contacts that Michael was a possible violent threat, and we feared for her safety," Grant explained. He looked over at Evelyn. "Having a recording of him slapping you lends a little credibility to the claim. It's probably an exaggeration, but if it get's us what we want..."

Evelyn smiled. "Fine with me. The sooner he's out of here the better."

"You're sure that she's coming alone?" Miranda asked.

Rose nodded. "Yes. I made sure to emphasize that you and Evelyn were going to be the only ones here. Something just for sisters."

"Do I need to leave?" Grant asked.

"You can stay," Evelyn told him. "You're too deeply involved in this anyhow, since you're the only other witness to what went on in the penthouse."

"That bastard. I can't believe he hit you," Rose said angrily. "I wish someone had made him pay."

"Well, I had to stop Grant from killing him," Evelyn said with an amused smile. "Pretty sure he would have done it too, if I didn't intervene."

"You should have let him."

"I'm sorry, but I don't want to have him stuck in a prison cell."

The conversation ceased as they heard the doorbell ring. Rose stood up.

"Wish me luck," she said.

He heard Miranda and Evelyn take deep breaths. The already tense atmosphere in the room seemed to grow more intense by the second. Grant grasped Evelyn's hand and squeezed it, trying to do something to reassure her. He felt her squeeze back.

Another voice broke the silence. "What's going-"

Grant turned around to see Josie enter the living room, a look of confusion on her face. Rose ushered her forward.

"We need to have a discussion," Evelyn said. "Without Michael here. That's why we told you that this was for sisters only."

"Oh..."

Grant watched Rose steer her sister to a seat, the shock still apparent. He wasn't sure whether to take that as a bad sign or not.

"Do you know what this is about?" Miranda asked gently.

"No. Why would I?"

"It's about the foundation. Particularly what your personal assistant has been doing to it. And by extension, you," Evelyn told her.

Josie suddenly stood up. "I'm sorry, I-"

Rose grabbed her by the shoulders and shoved her back down. "You're not going anywhere. Not until we get this straightened out."

"But-"

"No buts."

"What's going on with it, exactly?" Evelyn asked. "I've gone over the files. I've seen a lot of money being filtered through a shell company and then sent to an account in the Cayman Islands. All under your name, so to all appearances it looks like you're embezzling it."

Josie looked down. "I know it does," she said quietly.

"But that's not exactly right, is it? What's going on?"

"I'm the one. I'm the one responsible," she mumbled.

"That's not true, and I know it," Evelyn insisted. "I know for a fact that Michael's the one responsible for this. He's the brains behind this. So how is this all happening? Is he just framing you, or are you involved?"

"He... he..."

"What is it?" Miranda asked.

Grant began to pick up on the dynamic. Rose was acting as the steady center, keeping everything moving and containing Josie. Miranda offered gentle, kind words and some form of comfort.

That left Evelyn with the unenviable task of playing the villain, asking the difficult questions and pressing for answers. He imagined it had to be tough on her.

"I... It doesn't matter," Josie said. She sounded cowed... almost broken.

"Josie, we're trying to help you," Rose spoke up. "We know what's going on, and we're going to do what it takes to fix it."

"But I... I..."

"Here's what we know," Evelyn said. "The money is being paid to a shell company. A shell company that was founded in your name six years ago. The embezzlement started three years ago, when Michael showed up. I know he's responsible because he admitted it to my face. So are you helping him, or is he doing this on his own."

Josie stayed silent.

Evelyn scowled. "Staying quiet isn't going to help you, him or anyone else. He's already under federal investigation, and he's about to be arrested."

Grant saw her eyes widen.

"No, you can't do that," she said.

"The wheels are already in motion. It's too late to stop them."

"But you can't if he's arrested, then-"

"Then he's going to attempt to frame you," Miranda finished. "We know that's the kind of hold he has over you."

"But you-"

"We can and we will," Evelyn cut her off. "I have a voice

recording of him admitting that he was the one responsible. So once again, are you involved? Or is it just him?"

Josie looked down at the floor again.

"If you know something then you should cooperate," Miranda said.

"Here's what I think," Evelyn said. "Stop me at any point if I'm wrong. This company was created as a business venture that you forgot about. Maybe it slipped your mind almost immediately, or maybe you had real intentions for it, but it was forgotten. Is this sounding familiar?"

Josie didn't respond.

"So Michael comes along three years ago, planning to use you as a springboard to get into the Arno Corporation."

"That's not true," she protested. "He-"

"What, do you actually think he loves you or something? Would someone who loves you do something like this? Just using you as a means to an end?"

Her statement felt like a gut punch, and Grant tried not to wince. Shame started to wash over him. He may hate Michael's guts, but was he any different from him? Could he claim any moral superiority when he had come here to do exactly the same thing? Only a few steps separated them.

"Evie..." Miranda said quietly. "I think-"

"I don't fucking care," Evelyn cut her off. "If she doesn't listen now then she's never going to hear it. He's using you. He admitted it to me. And you know that, don't you?"

"That's a lie," she protested weakly. "He-"

Evelyn placed her phone on the coffee table and played

the recording. The others went completely silent, but the tension in the room only seemed to grow.

"So there you have it," Evelyn said. "You're a means to an end. Is it really worth protecting him?"

And then Josie began to cry.

Grant watched awkwardly as Rose and Miranda moved to comfort her. Evelyn stayed seated on the couch. He reached out to put a reassuring arm around her…

And he felt her trembling. Was it anger? Grief? Fear? Something else? Her expression remained stoic, but she definitely wasn't above it all. He felt her grab at his hand, putting it in a tight, almost crushing grasp. Grant squeezed back gently.

Miranda looked over at her unhappily. "I think you went too far."

"Better too far then to let her stay with him," Evelyn said. She looked back at Josie. "I didn't play all the recording. There was more. When I tried to leave he hit me."

Josie looked at her. "Oh."

"You don't seem surprised."

Josie looked down again.

"Has he hit you before?" Evelyn asked gently.

"It was only once. Twice, maybe. He apologized. He said he was sorry, that his anger got the better of him and he wouldn't do it again. He…"

Josie started to cry again, and Grant felt the rage boil up inside of him. If only he could get his hands around Michael's neck again, he…

"You're crushing my hand," Evelyn murmured in his ear, and Grant suddenly realized he was grasping far too tightly.

"Sorry," he said, releasing his grip.

"Maybe I should have let you throw him off the tower."

"I'm thinking that too."

"Yeah."

"If he hurt you then you can't just hide it," Miranda told her. "You need to let it go. He needs to pay for hurting you."

"You can get out," Rose said. "Testify against him."

"I can't. Please, just make it..."

"It's not going away," Evelyn insisted. "And I'm not going to let him near you to hurt you ever again. He's going away for a long time."

"But..."

"If he forced you to do it then you can testify against him. Don't let him hurt you any more than he already has."

"That will never happen again," a new voice said.

The four Arno sisters looked at the hallway in surprise. Grant took a glance as well, though he already knew who it was. He had asked him to come, after all.

Robert Arno walked into the room and strode over beside his eldest daughter. He put a hand on her shoulder and leaned down beside her.

"Sweetheart, I'm going to make sure that he never hurts you again."

Grant stood next to Evelyn's window and looked down at the entrance plaza as federal agents led Michael away, his hands cuffed behind his back. For some reason he felt a bit hollow watching the scene unfold. Maybe it was because he thought he was getting off too easy.

"So, interesting surprise you had in store for me," Evelyn commented.

Grant simply looked back at her and shrugged.

"Don't give me that. I never told you to contact my father about this. So why do it?"

"Honestly? Because I thought it was the best idea," Grant said. "I know you don't have a high opinion of him, but he's not going to let something like this go on and hurt one of his daughters."

"So you're saying he was your trump card?"

"You could say that, yes."

"Or are you just trying to put another feather in your cap?"

Grant turned around and looked her in the eye. "That's a low blow. Do you really think I'd sell you out like that? I promised that I wouldn't."

"And you still broke it."

Grant shook his head. "If you can't see the difference..."

She sighed. "I do. I don't have to like it, though."

Grant looked back out of the window. "I hope everything else turns out alright."

"Who knows if it will. I would have liked it if we could have made more progress with Josie, but..."

"But sometimes its hard to break away from a bad situation like that," Grant finished for her. "I know that all too well."

Evelyn nodded. "I know it's not a fairy tale. It's going to take time for her to make the break from him, if she ever does. It's not just going to magically happen. But still..."

"You may have started that break, at least," Grant said. "I know that was hard on you."

"It needed to be done," she shrugged.

"That doesn't mean it didn't hurt."

"Of course not. But there weren't very many choices. If I had to hurt her in order to help her, well..."

"Sounds like you're being a white knight yourself," Grant said lightly.

Evelyn gave him a sad smile. "I don't feel so noble right now, though. I'm honestly afraid that I hurt her more."

"You did what you thought was best. That's all you can do. That's all I could do."

"I know. Doesn't mean I have to like it."

"Which one? Your decision or mine?"

"Yes."

For some reason that made him smile. "Can't keep you down for long."

"I've learncd to roll with some pretty bad punches. This isn't much different from them," she replied. "I-" She stopped speaking as her phone went off. "Hello?"

Grant saw her frown.

"Understood," she said, and hung up.

"What was that about?"

She gave him a look. "That was my father. He wants to see both of us."

"Thank you both for coming on such short notice," Robert said to them as they entered his office.

Grant took a quick look around. It wasn't much, just a few pieces of furniture and some decorations, along with the same walls and black marble floors that filled the rest of the tower. He imagined that it probably wasn't used much.

"What did you want?" Evelyn asked.

"There's something I needed to discuss with both of you, and I wanted to do it as soon as possible."

"Oh?"

"Yes." He looked at Grant. "Your performance investigating the foundations was quite good, truth be told. The ending was a bit unfortunate, but none of that is your fault. You did the best you could in a bad situation."

"I had a lot of help," Grant said. "And I'm sorry that I could do more."

"You got the ball rolling at least, son, and that's all I can ask of you. Whether my daughter cooperates with the authorities or not is out of your hands. But you at least gave her a chance."

"Is there anything more?" Evelyn asked.

"Of course. Having such a good performance under his belt means that things can move faster than originally planned. I'm sorry to spring this on you now, Evelyn, but I want to move him into a proper position in the corporation."

Grant thought he saw her stiffen a bit, but maybe that was his imagination. Her expression remained the same.

"I suspected that was going to happen at some point," Evelyn said. "But tell me the truth. Was this all so you could hold him here in reserve?"

"It was."

"I thought that as well."

He turned to Grant. "Well son, there you have it. You'll be moved up into a financial advisor position in the Arno Corporation under my personal recommendation. That will put you in Dallas."

"I see," Grant nodded. He paused for a moment. "Won't this be trouble? I'm still carrying a lot of the burden from my last failure. I'd think that a lot of people in the corp. are going to be skeptical of me."

"People can be very forgiving of mistakes if you can do something for them in the present," Robert said. "And I think the job you did on this internal investigation is enough to dispel most of the issue. If anyone gives you trouble, let me know."

"I see."

"So what's your decision, son?"

What was his decision? In only a few short months he had been plucked from the abyss and had redemption straight in front of him. All he needed to do was to reach out and take it. Just grasp it in his hands. But…

"It's… a lot to take in right now," Grant said, trying to

stall for some time.

"Of course."

"It's what you wanted," Evelyn said.

Grant tried not to wince. That was the last thing he wanted to hear from her right now. Once again the feelings of shame washed over him. Could he really leave her here like this, even if she was expecting it? Could he just walk away and abandon her like all the rest?

"I can see this is going to be a tough decision for you, son," Robert said. "Very well. I don't want you coming into Arno with regrets on your mind. I'll give you a week to decide whether you want to take the position or not."

"Thank you sir," Grant said, feeling a wave of relief.

"Let me say this, son. You're talented, just like I've told you in the past. You have potential. You seem to have learned from your mistakes in the past. You have everything you need to be great in this world. All you need to do is reach out and take it, and I'm more than happy to give you that opportunity."

"Thank you."

He turned to Evelyn. "And this may put you in a difficult spot, having to find a new assistant on such short notice."

"It's fine. I'll manage."

For some reason that comment hurt him even more. The way she said it, so casually, so flippant, so... coldly. Maybe she was right. Maybe he'd never be able to get past the wall that surrounded her, and that he should move on if given the opportunity. It was right in front of him, waiting.

But...

"Well, that's it from me. I'll let you go so you can consider the decision. Oh, and son?"

Grant looked back at him. "Yes?"

"I'll have my number sent to you so you can call me when you make your decision. I'm flying out in a few hours, so you won't be able to give me an answer in person."

"Understood. Thank you again."

But what would that decision be? The question dogged him as he followed Evelyn out of the office. To stay or go? To follow his goal, or turn aside for something else?

Opportunity had come knocking for him, and Grant felt like it had just punched him in the chest.

Grant wrestled with his thoughts the rest of the day and came no closer to a resolution. Everything in his mind swirled together in a blur. He couldn't come to a decision, couldn't even think straight. What was the right choice? Was there even a right choice?

Nighttime swept over the tower. Grant sat in the shadows and continued to ponder his options. He had the opportunity he had come for right in front of his face, just waiting for him. Evelyn was expecting it to happen this way. She had said so from the beginning, and she continued to tell him that.

And if he stayed he might throw away his only shot at redemption. Even if he stayed with her she might never open up to him. Evelyn had told him point-blank that was the case. She had told him that the wisest course of action was to move on, to chase his goals and dreams.

So why did he feel so rotten about even considering leaving?

Do you love me?

"I don't even know you," he muttered to himself in response.

He didn't. He really didn't. Even after all the time spent together, even after an intimate, physical relationship with her he didn't truly know or understand her. What was waiting under the exterior she had shown him? Would he like what he saw, or would it give him pause? Would he even get to see it?

Grant's phone suddenly went off, startling him back to reality. He looked down at the text message.

Come to my room.

Grant sighed and texted back a message.

Do I need to since he's gone?

He thought since Michael was no longer a threat he would be back to sleeping in his own room. If he took the position he'd be gone soon enough anyhow.

His phone buzzed again.

Please.

Grant sighed again and stood up, heading for her suite. She certainly know how to cut deep when she wanted. In fact, Grant couldn't remember the last time she had asked him like this. Normally her requests were more like demands.

"You came," Evelyn said when she met him at the door of her suite.

"Of course I came," Grant told her. "You asked me to, after all."

"I wasn't sure after your response. I..."

"What do you need from me?" Grant asked her gently.

She took a breath. "I want you here with me. That's all."

"For the night?"

"Yes."

"Do I need to? With Michael gone..."

Grant's voice trailed off. Evelyn wrapped her arms around him and buried her face in his shoulder.

"Please," she murmured to him. "Just stay with me tonight."

He stood for a moment, then wrapped his arms around her in an embrace. "I will."

19

She wouldn't let go. Even as she slipped his clothing off she kept a grip on him, only releasing him for a split second before grasping him again.

Grant felt the touch of her skin as she removed the last of his clothing and embraced him.

"What's gotten into you?" he asked.

"What's that supposed to mean?"

"The last time you were like this..." he started to say, then trailed off.

She sighed. "It's not like that. Not this time."

"What's different?"

"It... it just is, OK? It's different from that time I tried to claim you. It's similar, but it's different too."

Grant frowned. "You're really not making sense. Are you saying that you're trying to claim me again?"

Evelyn looked away. "Maybe..."

"Didn't you say that-"

"Just let me pretend, OK? Just give me this."

He gave her a smile. "OK. I will. Whatever you want."

"What happened to you complaining about being forced to do things?"

"It's different than last time."

Evelyn laughed and gave him a light shove. "I guess I walked right into that."

"Yeah you did. But I'll still do whatever you want me to."

"Just… just be with me."

"OK?"

She lay down on her back. "I'll let you decide what we're doing. Let's see what you can do."

Grant laughed.

Evelyn gave him a look. "What?"

"That's what you said our first time," he said. "I don't know why, but it just made me laugh for some reason."

She smiled again. "Now that you mention it, I do remember saying that. But hopefully you're a lot more agreeable now than you were back then."

"I'd say so."

"Good. Now are you just going to keep me waiting?"

Grant leaned over and kissed her. He felt her sit up and grip his back keeping her lips locked onto his all the while.

"Ah. That had some passion behind it," she commented when they broke away.

"Why wouldn't it?"

"Well, I was the one that was claiming you."

"Yeah, but I let you do it."

"So you did like it," Evelyn grinned at him.

Grant looked away and didn't give her a reply.

"That's a yes."

"No, it's not."

"Oh, don't be so sour over it. I guess you just changed, that's all."

Grant looked back down at her. "You have too."

"I'm not so sure about that," Evelyn replied. "But I enjoyed having you here, at least." She reached up and gave him a kiss of her own.

Grant ran a finger down her spine, hearing Evelyn let out a soft moan in his ear. He swept the finger back up the same path, stopping at her neck and stroking his hand through her hair. All the pressure, all the cares in the world seemed to fade away. Right now the two of them were the only ones that existed.

Evelyn let out a louder moan as he slipped a pair of fingers between her legs.

"Not wasting any time, are you?" she sighed.

"I'll go as slow as you want me to," he whispered into her ear.

"It's your choice. Mmph. Wow, you're really going at it."

"I aim to please," Grant told her, feeling her getting wetter and wetter by the second.

He felt Evelyn grab for his cock and stopped her.

"I'm just-"

"It's fine," Grant told her, moving his hand and pulling her thighs apart. He let out a satisfied grunt as he slid inside of her.

Evelyn looked up at him with a smirk. "Huh. Couldn't wait, could you? Are you sure you're going to be able to last?"

"I'll make it work," Grant told her. He thrust, slowly at first, then picking up speed.

She sat up slightly, wrapping her arms and legs around his back. The suddenly shift in weight almost made him fall, but Grant steadied his body and pushed himself back into a seated position.

"Good recovery," Evelyn said.

"Warn me next time."

"Oh, where's the fun in that?"

He wrapped his arms around her and pulled her close, feeling her breasts press into his own chest. He could feel her breathing hard, feel his own heart pounding, feel the heat, the sweat, the urgency, taste her skin as he kissed her neck and shoulders, hear her soft moans...

He wished he could stay locked in this moment forever.

And then it was over too quickly.

"So how did I do?" Grant asked her, his chest still heaving from exertion.

"Good. You did good," Evelyn told him with a smile. She slid off of him and lay back down on the bed.

"You're not just saying that?"

"Hah. If you didn't actually satisfy me then I'd be on top of you riding you right now."

"I guess that's true," Grant agreed, lying down beside her.

"Oh, you know it is."

"Yeah." He looked away for a moment, then turned back to her. "You seem… different tonight?"

"Oh?"

"Yeah, like, I'm not exactly sure how to describe it, but…"

"Maybe you're just imagining things," Evelyn said.

Grant frowned. Her tone was a little too flippant for his liking, and it was also in complete contrast to how she had acted earlier.

"Are you trying to keep me from going?"

"What makes you say that?"

He tried to phrase his response as delicately as possible. "It just seems like you're holding onto me. I know what you said, but…"

"But you think that I'm still trying to hold you here, despite all of that," she said with a frown. "Is that what you think?"

Grant shook his head. "It's just an observation. I could be wrong."

"But if it was true, would that make you unhappy? Would you resent that?"

He went silent for a moment, trying to come up with a good response. Too many contradictory feelings were swirling around inside his head. He wanted to move forward, to redeem himself, but…

But was it worth it, especially when he might have something better wait for him here? Or was that even the case?

"I don't know," he said. "I just don't."

"I see."

He looked her in the eye. "And how do you feel about this?"

"Like I said, it's what you wanted. You need to do what's best for-"

"I don't care about that. I care about what you think. What are you going to do if I leave for this?"

Evelyn smiled at him, though it did nothing to put him at ease. Grant could tell that there was some sadness behind it. She concealed it well, but she couldn't erase it completely.

"I'll manage. Always have. But I'll be glad that you were able to get an opportunity. You deserve one."

"But-"

"But nothing." She suddenly rolled over onto him with a mischievous grin. "Ready for round two?"

"How many rounds are you planning on tonight?"

"Until one of us drops out," she told him. "Unless you don't think you'll be able to keep up? Puppy."

"That again?"

She laughed. "That got a rise out of you. So do you think you can handle it?"

"Of course I can."

Evelyn laughed. "Let's see if you actually can."

Grant spent the next day alone in his room, still trying to decide the best course of action. The previous night had only made his choice even harder. He still couldn't get a proper reading of Evelyn's feelings.

And what did he even think? She had told that he needed to think of himself, but what was the best choice? The new position offered a clear path, certainty that he had been craving for so long. But the other choice…

He looked up as his phone suddenly went off. Evelyn had sent him a message.

Meet me in the penthouse.

Grant quickly headed for the elevator, wondering what she had in store for him. Why the penthouse instead of her suite? Was there something else going on?

As soon as the elevator opened he hurried to the double doors. Evelyn was waiting for him inside, looking out the window into the night below.

"Thanks for coming up so quickly," she said.

"What, did you think I was going to wait around?"

"No, but I couldn't be sure."

"What did you need me for?"

Evelyn turned around. "We need to talk."

"About what?"

"About last night. About what your decision is."

"I still haven't decided yet," he told her. "I still have a few days to make it."

"I know. And that's what concerns me. You're too caught up in this."

"Meaning?"

"I can tell that you're split," she said, looking back down out of the windows. "You can't decide whether you should take the position, or whether you should stay here."

"I am," he admitted.

"Or maybe more accurately, you're split between chasing the goal you came here for versus staying here and trying to help me. Isn't that right?"

Grant stayed silent for a moment. "I wouldn't say that's it, exactly."

"You're lying," she said gently. "I'm not say that as an accusation. I'm just saying that's what I'm seeing from you right now. The biggest obstacle in your path is the fact that you don't think you can leave me like this."

"Can you blame me?" Grant said.

"I don't know. I'm not sure what to think at this point. I told you that it was going to be hard to open up to you. I told you at the beginning that I knew this was just a stepping stone for you. And nothing's changed since then."

"Nothing's changed..." he said, slowly clenching his fists. Her statement made him angry, for some reason.

"It hasn't," Evelyn said, turning around. "I don't know what y-"

"Now who's the one lying?" Grant said, looking her in the eye. "You can't tell me that nothing's changed. What was last night? What were all the times you started clinging on me?"

She sighed. "I knew you were going to bring that up. And I'm sorry if I sent the wrong message. But..."

Grant suddenly felt like someone had stabbed him in the gut and was slowly twisting the knife even deeper.

"So that's it? It was nothing to you?"

She looked at him with a hurt expression. "No. That's not it. But it was a moment of weakness on my part, and I'm sorry."

"Sorry? Why? Why should you feel sorry for that?" Grant said, feeling even more anger boiling up inside of him.

"Because it's misleading you. Because it's misleading me," Evelyn said. "It might have given me a taste of something that I know can never happen, and it's going to make me push your toward things that aren't in your best interests."

"Meaning you'll try to make me stay." Grant said quietly. "And you think that's the wrong decision. Why?"

"How many times do I have to tell you this? I can try to open up to you, but I have no idea if I'm even capable of doing that," she said, the anger in her own voice becoming apparent. "And then what happens? What happens to me when you decide you've had enough and leave? What happens to *you*? You'd have thrown away your best shot at redemption for something that you don't even know will be possible."

"What the hell."

"I know it's not-"

"What the hell?!" he exclaimed, his anger bursting forth uncontrolled. "Is this it to you? That you're just a commodity, a piece that gets weighed against a bunch of others? That you think you're less valuable than a position? What the hell? What am I supposed to think about that?"

"It's the way of things," she shrugged.

"In what kind of fucked up world is that true?"

"The world that we're living in right now, that's what," she snapped. "Do you really think that I like it this way?"

"So you're just going to let it happen instead of trying to change it? Is that what you really want?" Grant asked. "What happened to the woman that's driven? The one that's willing to push forward and fight for what she wants?"

Evelyn looked away. "She's an illusion, I guess. Maybe a figment of your imagination. I guess under all the bluster and bravado she's just a scared little girl, jumping at shadows and afraid of getting hurt."

"You really believe that, don't you?"

She looked at him with a sad smile. "Well, here it is. The woman that spent all that time leading you around by the collar and dominating you is scared by her own shadow. I'm really not worthy of standing beside you."

That last comment touched off a nerve deep inside of him. Grant felt another wave of anger boil up inside of him. How could she be so... casual, so accepting of her current plight?

"If you're a scared little girl, then I guess I'm nothing more than a scared little boy," he said. "Too stubborn to move on to something different, too needy for the praise of others. So I keep doing everything trying to get their approval."

"I see what you're doing," Evelyn said. "Don't. I'll be-"

"Don't say that you'll be fine. Don't."

"What do you want me to do, then? What should I do? Just keep holding you back? Hold you here for the slim hope of something that might never come true?"

Grant looked at her again. "You can't even hope and dream?"

"I did. But..."

Something clicked in his mind. "So that's it. That's what last night was. A way for you to pretend that you could have what you wanted. The thing that you can't have, or at least that's you believe, right?"

Evelyn couldn't meet his gaze. "Yes, that's why."

"If it's so important to you, then why aren't you at least willing to fight for it?"

"Because it's not really what I want."

Grant shook his head. "You can't tell me that. Not when I know you're lying."

She sighed. "This is what I was worried about. You want to be the white knight. My champion, or whatever. You want to ride in to save the day. And maybe I'd like that. But..."

"But what happens when I can't break down the wall. Yes, I know," Grant said.

"You can't just stay here and keep chasing dreams that

are never going to come true. Not when there's an opportunity waiting right in front of you. You have to reach out and take it. You'd be a fool not to."

"And what about you?" Grant demanded.

"I'll manage. I always have. I always will," she said.

Grant clenched his fists at his side and said nothing.

"But I will say this. You made my life a little more interesting, if only for a short time. And I think that was good for me."

"That's not what I want to hear," Grant said quietly.

"I'm sorry," Evelyn replied. "I really am. But I don't think I'm going to be able to give you what you want, and I can't keep you here for a slim hope that it's going to come true."

"So that's it, then? Are you just sending me away like that? I don't even get a choice?"

"Of course you do. It's your choice, just like always. But I don't want you to make a choice that you're going to regret later."

"What do you want me to do?"

"It's not about that. It's about doing what's best for you. And right now walking away might be the best course of action."

"I still have to think about it," Grant said, turning to go.

"Just… just don't do anything that you're going to regret later," Evelyn told him. "Don't make yourself a martyr for my sake. I'll be fine."

"You're just saying that."

"I'm not. Honest."

She might believe that, Grant thought as he walked away. If only he could.

He couldn't sleep. Grant tossed and turned all night, catching only an hour of rest here and there. The rest of the time he lay awake, watching the hours tick by slowly. The looming decision still haunted him. What should he do?

The sun loomed over the horizon, and dawn broke. Still, he couldn't come to a decision. Evelyn's words still haunted him. Grant thought that maybe he was breaking through to her. He had *felt* it when he was with her, but yet…

But yet she had chosen to retreat back behind the safety of the walls she had built around her, trying to keep from getting hurt again. His previous two attempts to reach out had failed. Why would a third, a fourth, a fifth attempt or beyond be any different?

Was she right? Was it better for him to move on, to grab the opportunity in front of him while he still had the chance? Grant had fought for years to make something out of himself, only to have it torn away by a betrayal. Now he finally had the chance to redeem himself. All he needed to do was reach out, take it for his own. Or he could stay for something that might never come to pass.

As the sun rose higher and higher into the sky he wrestled with the decision, pondered, agonized until he thought his head was about to burst. His heart felt heavy in his chest, almost like it was made out of solid rock.

Grant knew what he had to do.

He reached for his phone on the nightstand, took a deep breath and dialed the number. He had made his decision. Grant could only hope that it was the right one.

"Hello?"

"Good morning sir," he said.

"Ah, good morning son. I assume you're calling me to give an answer about the position?"

"I am."

Grant felt his heart pounding in his chest, his stomach turning in knots. Doubt started to creep into his mind. Was this the right call? Would this be something he would regret later?

No, he thought to himself, this was the right choice. This was the choice he needed to make. Evelyn was right. He needed to think about his own well-being, his own good. He couldn't just stay here out of a sense of duty or pity. He had chase his hope, his dream, even if that meant giving up something else that he valued greatly. There were some things more important than certainty.

Grant took another deep breath to steady his nerves.

"I'm sorry sir. But I'm going to have to decline your offer."

About the Author

Website
www.jsunpark.com

Facebook
https://www.facebook.com/authorjsunpark/

Twitter
https://twitter.com/authorjsunpark